THE SALT LETTERS

W9-AWH-043

THE
SALT LETTERS

Christine Balint

W. W. Norton & Company

NEW YORK   LONDON

First published in 1999 by Allen & Unwin, Australia
Copyright © 1999 by Christine Balint
First American edition 2001
First published as a Norton paperback 2001

The project has been assisted by the Commonwealth Government through the Australia
Council, its arts funding and advisory body.

All rights reserved
Printed in the United States of America

For information about permission to reproduce selections from this book, write to
Permissions, W. W. Norton & Company, Inc., 500 Fifth Avenue, New York, NY 10110

The text of this book is composed in Garamond 3 with the display set in Centaur
Composition by Sue Carlson
Manufacturing by Courier Westford
Book design by JAM Design
Production manager: Leelo Märjamaa-Reintal

Library of Congress Cataloging-in-Publication Data

Balint, Christine.
The salt letters / Christine Balint.
p. cm.
Includes bibliographical references.
ISBN 0-393-32160-6 (pbk.)
1. Women immigrants—Fiction. 2. Ocean travel—Fiction.
3. Young women—Fiction. 4. Australia—Fiction. I. Title.

PR9619.3B314 S25 2001
823'.914—dc21   00-068695

W. W. Norton & Company, Inc., 500 Fifth Avenue, New York, N.Y. 10110
www.wwnorton.com

W. W. Norton & Company Ltd., Castle House, 75/76 Wells Street, London W1T 3QT

1 2 3 4 5 6 7 8 9 0

*For all the immigrants whose
narratives provided the inspiration
and information for this book.*

*W*hen you step from the doors of Birkenhead Depot with your trunk, the ocean stretches before you. The sound of human sobbing is drowned out by the sound of screaming gulls. Once you have glanced at the sea, you never turn your head. From Birkenhead, the water appears thick grey. You move away from colour towards the horizon where sea and sky merge. It is always windy. Even in August you would reach to pull the cloak tighter around your waist.

Your limbs are numb as one of the officers helps you aboard the small boat. You try not to meet the eyes of the other women, while sitting so close that you feel their chests expanding with air. The officers joke as they begin to paddle. Freezing spray spits in your face.

You step aboard the vessel and it rocks violently. Its naked masts reach up to the heavens and are swallowed by the grey. The smell of fresh paint mingles with salt. Already you can hear creaking.

As you gaze at the shore at Portsmouth for the last time, firm fingers grip your arm and push you towards stairs leading down beneath the water.

Bay of Biscay
June 24, 1854

1. Mrs Louisa Garnett
c/- Frederick Garnett, Esq.
'Farraways'
Dorrington
Shropshire

My dear Mother,
It is difficult . . .

OUR BEDS ARE made on two raised platforms, one above the other, two feet apart. Lying side by side there are two to a bed. Even so, only a thin slat of wood separates each pair from the other girls. Our toes point towards the dining table at the centre of our mess. I share my bed on the bottom bunk with Annie. We have a Donkey Breakfast Mattress, which scratches like dry grass. It is brown and smells like dust. It is not soft and swollen like the one I had at home, but thin and worn as though rubbed bare by too many bodies.

Some people on board say our mattresses are filled with the clothes of drowned women. The stuffing gathers in lumps in the corners. When I woke last night to find Annie wrapped in our sheet, it was only the coarseness beneath my nightdress that reminded me I had any padding at all. At night the hatchway door is locked. An oil lamp smokes the wood of our berths.

Annie is thin and pale with long arms and legs. Her greasy hair reaches her waist. Her breath smells like castor oil and she presses her lips tightly together as though she has swallowed something bitter. Or to stop her secrets spilling forth. Annie sucks my air and breathes empty words into the darkness. She reminds me of an octopus: her tentacles tangle around my neck and wrists. These last two days I have not seen Annie smile and she rarely speaks to anyone.

I am violently awoken during the night, landing on the floorboards at the foot of my bed. My head swells with thought just as the boards swell with moisture. Perhaps if I were to lie on my stomach with my right hand underneath the mattress, I could prevent being flung into the air and bruising my skin on the beds above. When I climb back into bed, Annie and I are tossed together like lamb's fry. Had I known it would be like this, I may not have come.

For two mornings I have woken to find Annie sitting next to me, clasping her knees to her chest, rocking even more than the vessel would make her. Her face muscles twitch and her skin is light green.

'We are still in England,' she moans. It is true. And I can feel the anchor beneath us, holding the vessel back when she would move. Yet we rock enough to find no peace even in sleep. We have all been weakened before our journey may begin.

It is possible that I am being granted time as a test of strength. I imagine waiting until the sighs of sleep fill the air around me, and hobbling barefoot to the cabin at the end where Matron sleeps. The light from the lamp above the hatchway would allow me to find my way. I would be careful not to fall too heavily against oak as the rocking vessel tried to toss me to the boards. I would feel Matron's petticoats for the key, swing about in alarm to hear her snort. Then the silver key around her neck would catch my eye. I am sure she sleeps heavily. Fat folds of skin under her chin and on her bosom anchor her to the world of dreams. She would not notice my fingers slipping the cord from around her neck.

This key would be the key to my escape. I would tiptoe to the hatchway and unlock the door, which flaps loudly even when fastened. The creaking would make no more noise than the creaking of the ropes, which has become our lullaby. The blackness of the sky, the salty air and the specks of starlight would grant me strength. On the deck I would bound towards the lights of Birkenhead, relishing the uncluttered space. I would fling the metal key into the bay and watch it disappear into the inky ocean. Then I would dive overboard. I know the sea would be cold and rough, and that my nightdress would tangle around my legs. But my arms would pull me towards the certainty of land.

Alone among the immigrants, we unmarried women are locked deep in the ship. We are in the rear section below the cabins; my mess is next to the married people's accommodation. I breathe faint lavender through the cracks in the wall, my ears ache with the sounds of people. I hear short sharp gasps of breath and airless giggling. The air has known us all intimately and is tired. It is as trapped within us as we are below the deck.

Each mess of girls has been assigned a constable. The constable is a married man whose job is to take food to the galleys to be cooked after it has been prepared by the captain of the mess. When the food has been cooked, the constable brings it back. Apart from our constable, Mr Greenwood, we will not see a man for days at a time.

Already I feel as though there is nowhere for me to go. I have no standing room to speak of and even my half-bed is constantly impinged upon. The berths are scattered with untidy articles of clothing and cooking implements. Since we have no drawers or cupboards there is nowhere to hide our belongings in pretence of tidiness. Our clothing forms irregular mounds in the canvas bags hanging from the bedposts.

Today we lie on our beds and stare up at the rough grey paint. Some of us gossip to each other when our stomachs allow speech. Others try to sing. I hear children running up and down the 'tween decks, chasing each other and making the boards tremble. A small boy peers into the unmarried women's accommodation as if to discover why we are so quiet when everywhere else is movement and noise. My mind has nowhere to rest.

They say we are awaiting the arrival of the captain. We are all curious to see who will guide us into the New World. We want to know how many times he has travelled there and returned. He alone will have the knowledge of what is there. But we worry that he will become mesmerised by the sea and will lose his sense of direction. That we shall be slashed to pieces and stripped of all that we possess by cannibals in Africa. We dare not speak of the wild men of the New World.

GRANDFATHER FRYER WAS a ship's captain. He liked to talk about currents, and said that they were determined by the temperature of the sea. He talked about a river of cold water flowing between layers of warm. The warm water was like veins for the cold sea blood. The oceans ruled the air.

It was said he had an internal compass that allowed him to navigate a vessel even in the most treacherous of conditions. He could be blindfolded, Mother said, and could still steer a ship away from sharp rocks. Grandfather Fryer said that at some points the ocean was so deep that its bottom could not be discovered. In fact, he said, we cannot even be sure that there is a bottom. The water may reach the centre of the earth. The deeper the colour, the higher the quantity of salt.

Grandfather Fryer spent some years at the salt works in France. He said that just before crystallisation the water turned crimson.

Grandmother Fryer was fond of sailors; she said they had the inconsistency of the ocean running through their veins. She was excited by their ripples. She relished the smell of salt on their skin and in their hair. Whenever Grandfather Fryer's vessel returned, Grandmother Fryer invited his sailors to stay. In the evenings they would drink gin and sing sea shanties while Captain Fryer read in his library.

⟜

IT IS THE third day and the cabin passengers have begun arriving. We hear their boots on the deck above our heads; gentlemen complaining over the lack of private room in which to wander and contemplate; women annoyed that they shall not be permitted access to their trunks until a month after departure. They do not appreciate that they have three days fewer to endure the swelling and dropping of the ocean. The cabin passengers arrive on little rowing boats. We hear small groups of musicians playing 'Rule Britannia'. It is as though they believe that if the music is loud enough, Britain will even be able to rule over the ocean.

We lie on our hard beds, in heavy contemplation of the months before us. I cannot believe I will survive the conditions of the voyage: the damp darkness below deck, the stagnant, rotting air. The preserved cabbage. People quarrelling over provisions. The constant noise: the groaning from the married people's accommodation, the children squealing and wreaking havoc on board, the sobbing and heaving of the other unmarried women. There is nothing to be of comfort.

As the afternoon begins to cool, we hear excited chatter but few words. A woman is weeping, a child screams. People below deck begin to mutter.

'The captain wishes to speak,' a man somewhere in the married people's accommodation says quickly, while women snap at their children that it is time to climb the hatchway stairs. My head sways as I try to stand. I wonder, suddenly, if there is a problem with the vessel and if we will be required to alight immediately to prevent drowning. Or if perhaps there is a criminal amongst us whose identity must be discovered before we are to leave England. It is possible that there are too many passengers on board and some of us must remain behind.

The matron, her eyes twitching behind her spectacles, begins to walk towards the hatchway. One of the girls moves from her bed and makes as though to follow her.

'Remain in your berth!' Matron orders. 'All that the captain wishes to say is not for your ears.'

Silence billows and drifts until it fills all the space below the poop. The unmarried women lie on their beds, some sniffing quietly and others trying to muffle their retching with handkerchiefs. As soon as Matron disappears from view, girls begin to whisper.

'Something is wrong!'

'We shall die of consumption!'

'We are all to be put in chains!'

The words of the captain, the ship's husband, stream through the flapping hatchway door and float in the stale air. Boards creak under the weight of boots. But words are swallowed by shrieking winds and the waves beating the vessel. Feet thump towards the sea and a man's voice shouts, 'I cannot!'

There is a muffled cry of 'Hurrah!' and the vessel lurches forward. She is free of Old England.

Now the water is still closer. Even in steerage where we cannot see the ocean, salt water foams and trickles down from the deck. A small ocean splashes tiny waves against our ankles and splatters our stockings. We try to mop the salt water from the boards before it seeps its way into our belongings; we dread that it will poison our treacle and stain our dresses with green mould.

Although it is only late afternoon, Matron has agreed that we may go to bed without supper if we wish. Even she is pale. I wonder if she has given us permission to rest so as to relieve herself of responsibility for our wellbeing and our whereabouts. It is certainly easier to endure the movement lying down. If I grip my arms around my stomach I can almost forget the muddy tea from lunch-time, burning the inside of my belly as it rises slowly upwards.

I try to talk to Annie. It is usual to converse, albeit briefly, with one's bedfellow before sleep. I ask whether her parents were distressed when she boarded to leave England. For some time she does not speak. She stares sullenly at the boards above our bed. I hold my breath and wonder if she will answer.

When she opens her mouth, the words are barely audible. 'Everyone was glad to see me go,' she murmurs.

'Do you know people in New Holland?'

'My brother . . .'

As I lie under my blankets, the creaking ropes echo in my head and already I wonder if we shall ever arrive. I hear the dregs of the sea washing in through the water closets. The ocean on our floorboards, even when it is fresh, is not blue but the colour of mud. It laps a quiet echo of the grand ocean beneath the vessel. Perhaps the water will cleanse the boards, ridding us of some of the dirt that finds its way into our quarters. I fear that soon steerage will fill with gushing water. With no one awake to keep an eye on the tiny sea, and only the faint light from the oil lamp above the hatchway, the ocean on the boards will rise until we are swimming in our beds. By then it will be too late to mop. We will have to wait while the vessel sinks and the water rises, lifting us upwards. There will be time to be afraid and time to pray. Finally we will float with barely enough space for our heads between the rising tide and the deck. Afterwards people will claim that the unmarried women sank the vessel.

The icy breeze wafts down cracks in the hatchway door and freezes my toes. There is a quiet time this evening, just after we have settled in for the night, when our stomachs cease heaving. But the illness remains within me, rocking from one side of my stomach to the other with the waves. The lamp near the hatchway is lit and flickers violently in the cold air. It gives off the faint odour of smoke, which, if I concentrate, can remind me of winter evenings in Father's library.

At night I long to go back there. A place ticking to the regular rhythms of the mantel clock. Where time is rigid and stories are captured in crisp leather-bound pages. Where nothing is foreign except perhaps the chess set William brought back from Edinburgh.

For all its peacefulness, the library held the sour, dusty smell of death. Polly once told me that dust was formed from the skin of dead people.

Everything on board the ship is alive. Death is thrown to the sharks.

GRANDMOTHER FRYER SMELLED of fish. She salted the air around her so that, during the summer, she was trailed by flies. People would wrinkle their noses as she walked past, and wonder whether it was possible that such a foul smell could emanate from the gentle old woman wearing the blue bonnet. It was said that Grandmother Fryer's diet consisted entirely of seafood. Mother frowned as she told me that my grandmother ate herrings for breakfast, mackerel for lunch and a baked cod or an occasional haddock for her evening meal. Her skin took on a silver shine and in her dreams she walked on the seabed. She used to suck the eyeballs of fish until they dissolved in her mouth. A friend of Captain Fryer's, who was a medical doctor, took a great interest in her and began to conduct secret experiments. It was said that she had developed the ability to breathe under water.

⁓

THERE IS A kind of madness in perpetual movement. It is never long before my mind begins to wander and I am distracted by all that surrounds me. I can do no more than begin letters to my mother. None of us are ever still and we can rarely walk two steps without being thrown from one end of our berth to another. I can control my direction no better than the boots I leave under my bed in the evening only to spend the following morning scouring the muddy boards to find them again. When my eyes are closed, the movement frequently makes me dizzy and ill. It is impossible to forget I am here.

The pitch of the sea becomes deeper as we move further from home. I sense the depth of the ocean by the depth of her voice. Now it is not a regular and steady slapping against the sides of the vessel, but a number of different voices constantly interrupting each other, whispering. During the night I make out words. I can almost ascertain the pitch of my name as the ocean sighs, 'Sarah. Sarah. Sarah.'

When the sea is particularly rough, our illness, in all its colours and textures, is washed into a colourful fluid that sloshes from one end of the vessel to the other. I have had to convince myself that it is specks of sea life and not softened husks of oatmeal or half-digested peas that have flowed from the mouths of my fellow passengers.

This morning Mrs Dawson's infant was scalded to death when a large wave hit as his mother was carrying a teapot. Doctor Carpenter said that this would be the first of many deaths on the voyage. He shook his head and said we should be grateful for our good health.

The first service was read by the schoolmaster. The child was wrapped in a canvas bag with a cannonball to make it sink. His body slid down a wooden plank into the sea.

The tiny ocean on the boards has many objects floating upon it. Pocket handkerchiefs sink to its grimy ocean bed. Tin cups are tossed and flung against each other. I have even spotted a small jar containing a letter that was probably intended to float all the way to the single men's accommodation.

My belongings make miniature voyages all of their own that I can only imagine and something has begun taking small bites from my skin. I have been dreaming about being stung by giant insects. And, indeed, I awake to find my arms covered in tooth marks.

It seems as though I am on an ark. On the quarterdeck there are three wooden sheds. One of them houses a cow who must provide milk for all the passengers. I have heard that Bessie has not yet discovered her sea legs and that there is fear she will not survive even the first half of the journey. She groans so loudly that if it were not for the fact that she must provide milk, I am sure she would become food for the captain's table. The smallest shed houses two pigs who have no room to do anything other than slurp up the remnants of our food. The tallest shed contains a mare. She has smooth round flanks and a matted mane. She thumps the floor of her shed with strong hooves and likes to peer over the top of her gate. The inside of her shed is walled with the skin of other horses, stuffed to appear as though heavy with life. They are intended to provide padding during the sudden lurches of the vessel and to supply company during the tribulations of the voyage. However, I am sure that the mare does not find comfort in the fur of dead horses.

There is a man on board known as 'Keeper' whose task is to feed the animals and muck out their byres. Keeper is also a clown. He delights in giving freedom to the pigs, and this afternoon he allowed them to roam freely in steerage for hours before any of the other passengers or crew discovered that the animals were missing from their shed. It was of some concern to the cabin passengers when the animals were gone only because they feared that they had been deprived of a hearty meal in which everyone else of importance had taken part.

Keeper also hands out rations to the immigrants, but since our rations are not given directly to us but to our constable, I have never met him. I imagine him to be small, thin and boyish in appearance. He must have the ability to move deftly and at great speed in order to release the pigs into steerage without Captain Coughin noticing.

It seems to have befallen the unmarried women to keep the animals from mischief. Mother would be horrified to learn that her daughter is sharing living quarters with a pig. Yet I am growing accustomed to her company. Since we left Portsmouth she has been well fed on the nourishment we are offered but remain unable to stomach. There is no comfort in food. The pork is so salted that she probably remains unaware of her cannibalism.

She is dusty pink with a small triangle of thin flesh missing from her left ear. The pig has been following Eliza, who is captain of the mess. She snuffles at Eliza's ankles before lifting her head to the sound of blunt knives sawing soft vegetables, as though expecting food to be thrown to her. The pig pushes her snout under a different girl's bed each evening she is in steerage. She likes to sleep in complete darkness but only her head will fit into the space at the foot of the bed. She is grateful for mud. We must all be careful during the night that we do not trip over her. Early in the morning she wakes and explores the berths while they are empty of life. She leaves long dark lumps of the most potent odour on the boards. Eliza has spent a number of hours trying to train the pig to relieve herself away from the beds, beneath the hatchway stairs. When we laughed at Eliza's earnest discussion, she glared. The pig was listening, she said.

'Can't you see her ears twitch? We must try to train her or we shall all be wallowing in filth for months.'

The pig, unlike the rest of us, wanders freely in steerage. If Eliza could train her to speak she would have many stories to tell. She would know from the different smells in the married people's accommodation and in the men's accommodation what they were eating. She would know how they pass the time and what they talk about.

The other pig has now been slaughtered for the saloon table. Quite a game the men thought it was. That was the only time they have been free to enter the unmarried women's accommodation, though Matron kept a very strict eye. Sly Bill came bustling through behind the table, just as Annie was removing her stockings. Annie squealed almost as loudly as the pig did, fearing for its life and ramming its head against the splintered leg of our dining table.

Sly Bill did not wait until they had removed the pig from our quarters before pulling out his knife and slashing the thick flesh around its neck. The pig continued to squeal until it was almost beheaded; a number of girls screamed and clutched each other. Hot blood flowed from the wound and ran in rivers down its flanks. The pig collapsed in a crimson puddle while steam rose to cling to our skin. Matron tried to shout, but it was several minutes before she was heard.

'William Green, this is not a slaughterhouse. You are never, never again to kill an animal in the unmarried women's accommodation. Now, take the creature away and clean up the mess.'

For days an orange-coloured ocean lapped at our feet. Every unmarried woman wore a dress rimmed with brown, her stockings splattered. All clothing beneath our ankles became tainted with blood and we learned to walk with clamped jaws in an attempt not to succumb to our disgust.

I am growing very fond of the remaining pig and have come to look out for her. I am aware, almost constantly, of whether she is in steerage or in her shed on the quarter-deck.

I have always had an extra sense of the location of my loved ones. Polly hated to play hide and seek with me because I always found her immediately. Yet I would often be reading the final pages of a book underneath the side-board before Polly appeared, enraged and exhausted after her search. If ever Mother was looking for William, she only had to ask me and I would know his whereabouts. Mabel took to consulting me about whether or not he would be returning in time for supper.

For a year before I left, I knew every minute where Richard was and when he was coming to see me. My sense of location was equally acute with those I feared. Whenever Mr Downing was coming to visit, I would feel ill as the time drew near, though I could only ever identify in hindsight that my illness had been from dread.

∼

YESTERDAY I WAS preparing mutton stew. I stood with my feet wide apart, trying to balance. I sometimes pretend to dance. If I stare in front of me for long enough, I can see the grey of Richard's eyes as he holds my hand shyly, careful not to grip too tightly. Waltzing with ghosts may stop me from falling.

Suddenly a large wave hit—I heard it crash on deck while someone up there called Cranky Jim swore a nasty oath. As the floor lurched, I fell against the table. Had the knife been sharper, I would have lost a hand. Instead, I gouged the skin. My hand is swollen mauve with a deep red split. I have tried to keep it hidden from Matron for fear of mustard. While it is painful now, I am afraid of that heavier, burning pain. If she notices, I know Matron will paint me in mustard like beef to draw out the infection.

When I was twelve and bedridden with consumption, the doctor marked my chest in brown paste that gave me vivid dreams. I was being swallowed by a flickering yellow flame. It was only when Florrie poured water on my face that I could pull myself from the dream and I fear that now I will be left alone to my visions.

~~~~~

MOTHER HAD GROWN up in the house with Grand-mother Fryer in Cornwall. Grandmother Fryer had passed on to her the secrets of womanhood and had waved proudly to Mother as she left her wedding on Father's arm. Mother had tried to ignore the drops of red wine on Father's crumpled jacket. She had tried to look away from Uncle Frederick and his wife, averting her eyes from his dry smile and neatly buttoned clothes.

'We will rarely meet again, now,' Grandmother Fryer

had winked at Mother, and turned to find Grandfather Fryer slumped over his empty plate and snoring with the regularity of crashing waves.

After I was born Mother began inviting Grandmother and Grandfather Fryer to stay. She wrote to them several times a year, but Grandfather Fryer was frequently absent and Grandmother Fryer at first said that she preferred not to make the journey from Cornwall alone. She wrote that she had come to think of herself as an oyster and that the wind and rain were welding her to the rocks. She needed Grandfather Fryer to prise her from the seashore, she said. Yet when Grandfather Fryer was at sea, no one ever knew where Grandmother Fryer was.

But during my ninth summer, Grandmother Fryer and the captain accepted Mother's invitation. Because she thought it was the right thing to do, Mother ordered soft-bodied creatures in coarse shells from the fishmonger in Shrewsbury. She instructed Mabel on the best way to pre-pare the meal, though Mabel could not become accus-tomed to cracking the shells. She whispered to me when Mother had left the kitchen, that they cracked like bones.

Florrie spent three weeks cleaning the silver. Polly and I embroidered small cushions covered in sails to welcome Captain Fryer to Shropshire. We had practised asking each other questions about grand voyages so that we would have topics to discuss with Captain Fryer on his arrival.

There was so much chatter when the grandparents arrived, that it seemed everyone spoke at once. Grand-mother Fryer waddled unsteadily, clutching a walking stick as though the weight of her long hair, plaited and pulled into a bun slightly off centre, put her off balance. She peered into my eyes. Captain Fryer took large, smooth steps. He beamed silently from behind his white beard, swaying from side to side.

William announced that he had thought about trying to become a sailor. Mother frowned. Grandfather Fryer did not discuss the life of a sailor, but instead began to tell William that he was excited about the trade winds. He said they grew from two points, 30 degrees latitude on both sides of the equator. They blew a huge circle into the atmosphere, controlling the climate of England, making it warmer than other parts of Europe and bringing rain and fog. These winds blew Englishness all over the world. They were responsible for civilising the earth.

⁓

SOME PLACES ARE never destinations. The path to church was never a place to stop, and would not have existed if it did not lead somewhere else. There were bushes that I did not look behind or forage underneath. There was so much green that filled in spaces.

Now there is blue which fills in ocean floors and covers mountain tops. The ocean has coated flowers and small animals like larva. It forces us to look at its surface while it blocks all that is underneath. Below the surface it is a black shadow, always changing shape but never lessening in density. I peer into the ocean and see the outlines of giant sea monsters that would swallow me whole. I could float between their teeth and they would not feel my presence. I see the remains of vessels and meandering paths on the ocean floor.

It is only a week since we left Portsmouth and I have heard that we lost our main anchor. The sailors were so distracted by the violent motion of the sea that they had forgotten to check the cable. The heaving of the ship caused the anchor to slide from the deck when it was not adequately fastened. I imagine the object sinking beneath the sea and becoming wedged in the seabed. It frightens me somewhat, for I feel that perhaps the anchor was supposed to stick and that the vessel was not meant by Providence to continue her journey. I fear there is danger ahead. Or that the sailors' carelessness will cause a catastrophe.

Captain Coughin was very angry and gave them a strict talking to. It is early on the voyage for the sailors to lose concentration. If anything like this happens again, the captain said a man will be locked in irons. Fortunately we were still crossing the Bay of Biscay and he managed to signal to a passing ship that we required a new anchor. It was delivered by two fishermen in a rowing boat that tossed so violently Doctor Carpenter feared they would not be able to return safely to land. The captain was annoyed that the new anchor was so expensive, but said that he would pay the additional cost since the men had been forced to endure such hazardous conditions to supply it.

ON THE FIRST evening of her visit, Grandmother Fryer lifted the walking stick that she had prevented Florrie from taking away from her. She waved it like a pointed finger in the air and demanded to be given a tour of the house by the Young Ladies. As Grandmother Fryer pulled herself up from the chair, Mother stood to catch her fall. Grandmother Fryer glared and startled Mother by poking her shoulder with the walking stick.

Grandmother Fryer demanded that Polly and I walk ahead of her towards our rooms, and said that she would follow. We were not to watch her, she said. We had to trust that she was there. Polly and I held hands, shuffling towards the nursery. Once there, we offered Grandmother Fryer a chair. We folded our pinafores behind our legs and knelt at her feet.

Grandfather Fryer was married to his vessel, she said. He was happiest in the arms of his ship because she never made demands on him and was comfortable with his long silences. 'A woman is more than a vessel,' Grandmother Fryer said, poking a doll's pram with her walking stick. 'Remember that.' I nodded, imagining myself lying on my back, one leg a rudder, the other foot a keel, my hands waving in the breeze like sails while I floated on an ocean.

Mother did not eat with us that evening. At the dining table, Grandmother Fryer used her fingers to pluck the jellied oysters from the shells. The creatures tasted like pure, wet salt and smelled as though they had been too long out of the ocean. I realised that it was only Grandmother Fryer who relished the food, sucking every last drop of salty water from her fingers.

To celebrate the arrival of the grandparents, Mother had decided that we would serve Groper Head and Shoulders Boiled. Mabel was anxious about cooking the fish, for she had heard that there is a great art to boiling a groper at the correct temperature to prevent the head from losing its shape. The fish appeared as swollen and as moist as if it had been placed directly on the platter from the sea. Mabel smiled to herself as she divided its gelatinous lips into equal parts.

After Grandmother Fryer had gone, Mother would not leave her room for days. She insisted on closing her door at all times. 'Sarah,' she said quietly, 'Grandmother Fryer is mad.'

Mother claimed that Grandmother Fryer had infected our air with the rancid smell of fish.

～⌐

WHATEVER I SWALLOW tastes of bitterness and salt. The lime juice I drink flows as quickly out of my mouth as it flows in. I can only be grateful that I rarely require the water closet. That is the surest way of dampening with salt water parts of one's anatomy that are usually covered. I fear I will rot in darkness. Or perhaps I will become dry and salted.

I often see Richard reflected in water. Yesterday I thought I saw his face in a pannikin. Occasionally, when the ocean at our feet is roughest, I expect him to burst up from the bowels of the ship almost like a mermaid, or to swim through the married people's accommodation. I imagine him laughing and running after me, splashing his way around steerage.

At certain times of the day there are queues to use the water closet nearest our berth. Straight after breakfast, there is a rush to go there first. Matron is most disapproving when we make our need to use the water closet apparent. She says that we should all remain ignorant of the bodily workings of other women. This is impossible when we spend so much time together that our bodies follow the same patterns. The other times when many women wish to use the water closet are before our evening meal and after drinking the rich black tea of afternoon. The water closet is a cramped space with wooden walls. When the door is closed, the light comes in thin horizontal shafts through the door. Matron says we must become accustomed to attending to our bodily needs in near darkness. She says it would not be proper to see what we are doing. Despite the discomfort of using the water closet, I have found that sometimes I need to go there as a means of escape. It is the only place on board the vessel where I cannot be seen. I go there to be alone when I know that the others are occupied and thus unlikely to require it. I sit upon the wooden plank as straight as possible and hold my hands against the wall, trying to keep still. I close my eyes and try to dream. If I am careful to go there mid-afternoon, there is no smell. However, it is possible to be very unlucky if a wave hits and someone has recently been using the water closet. It is certainly never long before water begins to spray up through its mouth.

At eight bells, the first mate makes it noon. We are not allowed to watch the calculations but Mr Greenwood has explained that a sextant is used to measure the elevation of the sun over the horizon. This means that at eight bells it is close to true noon. But often I do not feel as though it is nearly lunchtime. I think back to those at home, and how not even time may link us any longer.

Two days ago there was trouble when the sandglass fell. Though it did not break, it was some time before anyone noticed. Until the clocks showed noon the following day and the first mate began his calculations with the sextant again, no one was sure of exactly what time it was. This caused Captain Coughin some concern. Matron also became alarmed and started shouting at the doctor that she needed to know the exact time if order and routine were to be preserved. The doctor gave her a drachm of laudanum to calm her nerves.

New friends made on board ship are called Dunkeys. I wonder which friends will be left when we arrive. We all have our own stories. That is how we began to each other. We now have few secrets. We must become to each other all the people we have left behind.

Eliza is the oldest in our mess. She is travelling to the New World following the death of her father. She kept house for him and has not married. Beth is going out to join her mother and stepfather who are living in Van

Diemen's Land. It is three years since Beth's mother and stepfather left for New Holland. She says that her stepfather shows far too much interest in her gentlemen friends. Beth hopes she will meet a suitable gentleman to marry soon, so that she will not have to live with her stepfather for very long. She often makes us laugh. At night Beth sometimes acts out a meeting with a young man. She wears a hat fashioned from paper when playing the part of the man and growls, 'Pleased to make your acquaintance, Miss,' in a deep voice.

Charlotte is travelling to the New World to marry a man she has not seen for two years. Her fiancé, Harold, is making his fortune in the Victorian Goldfields. Charlotte says she is excited at the prospect of a life built upon the security of gold. We are all invited to the wedding, which is to take place shortly after arrival.

⁓

I WAS TEN on the day Richard first arrived with Uncle Frederick. Uncle Frederick seemed much older than Father. His body was shrunken and his face framed with deep grooves. He trembled as he reached for Mother's hand to greet her. His eyes were faded. He and Mother retired to the drawing room. We took Richard to the nursery. After Uncle Frederick had gone, Mother shook her head and held a forefinger to her nose. 'He has had a hard life,' she whispered.

William and I had been so excited at the visit from our cousin that we did not realise until evening that Father had not greeted his own brother. In fact, it was as though Father had remained unaware of our guests. He did not emerge from his cellar until supper.

During the meal, Father behaved as though Richard had always lived with us. He glared at my brother and my cousin as they mashed their carrots with forks and giggled like young women. He shook his head at Polly, who was singing through half-chewed roasted potatoes. He paid Richard as little attention as he paid William, Polly and myself. Perhaps even less.

～～

MATRON SAYS WE all require discipline if we are to survive in the New World. At seven we are woken; we rise to sand the boards and eat breakfast. The performance of breakfast is unnecessary since most of us are still too sick to eat, and at least one person is scalded with tea or wounded with a knife at each meal.

We cannot do our own work because we are thrown so suddenly that it would be dangerous to use a needle. But Matron says there is much work to be done during the voyage. She informs us that fabric and coloured cottons have been generously donated by respectable charities. If we are well behaved, we may be given our own needle-work on arrival. Then we shall colour our real cottages with the cotton we have stitched.

I close my eyes and try to picture a cottage that would be my own. I can see the cobbled streets of Shropshire or the busy shopfronts of London Town, but I cannot imagine a cottage in a place without roads. I try to sketch the knobbed trees with dusty grey leaves and twisted branches that I have heard about, but they dissolve back into my mind. I worry that it will be hard to protect ourselves from savages and the wild prisoners. I will probably need to learn how to use a gun. Father would be disappointed that my life could force me to protect myself. I remember the days when he and Mr Downing went shooting while I remained behind with Mother and Polly.

The strain of trying to pull my thoughts from the voyage makes my temples throb. I cannot imagine for long because the rocking of the vessel tips any other thoughts from my mind. At present we are unable to spend our days productively. I pray each morning and evening for calmer weather.

The fish I swallowed when I was in the river is making me tired. I wonder if anyone can see my belly twitch with its motion. I imagine that it is a rainbow-coloured fish growing long and beautiful inside me where it cannot be harmed by hooks or rocks. I wonder if I should tell someone about the fish because I know it will eventually be freed from my body. Whenever I am ill, I fear that the waves of my blood will spew the fish from my mouth and that the others will be alarmed when they discover it flapping on my bed.

The sailors call the deck the Monkey Poop. It is too wet and slippery for us to be allowed up there for any length of time. I have heard Beth and Charlotte whispering about the monkey poop. Beth says she is going to meet one of the sailors up there at midnight under the stars when we are all asleep. I told her that she was mad even to think of such a thing, that if she didn't slip and break her neck, Matron would catch her and boil her up for breakfast. Besides, I told her, Mr Greenwood informed me that the stars and moon are presently smothered in thick, smoky clouds.

It is very difficult to work out the time in steerage where day is almost as black as night. But I am growing more accustomed to assessing the quality of the light through the cracks in the hatchway door. I find it nearly impossible to sleep on this vessel. At night, when my mind is becoming lighter, Eliza tucks my blankets tightly under the thin mattress. Lately she has begun to whisper her stories before she returns to her own bed.

Eliza says it was anger that forced her to leave England. I find this difficult to believe for I have never seen her angry. She says her feelings became so strong that she was rigid. She could barely move her limbs from stiffness and her head ached because her jaw was always clamped. She wonders how it is that someone could find herself so unsuited to the very environment and circumstance into which she was born and in which she has always lived. The longer Eliza stayed in England, the more furious she became with the people who surrounded her and their expectations, until she felt that she had to leave. 'Even if I do not survive this voyage,' she says, 'it is still a good thing that I have left England, because with the shores of the Mother Country I have left my bitterness behind.'

Eliza's father was a charitable doctor who struggled to feed his family. He believed that Eliza should follow her destiny and that she was born to be a painter. Eliza believed this herself, and knew that she was never happier or calmer than when she had her watercolours and her blanched white paper before her. Eliza's simple cooking provided adequate nourishment for the family. And every few months, her father would appear after work with a surprise gift of a new paintbrush or some fresh colours.

But when Eliza turned eighteen, the attention of the other women in the town turned to her. It happened that there were far more young men than young women in the town, and although she was not wealthy, as the daughter of the doctor she would make a suitable wife. Young men frequently called in the evenings. Eliza's father would welcome them as his guests and invite them to stay to supper. After the meal, Eliza grew impatient for them to leave. The more persistent ones would ask her for a stroll and, in the beginning, Eliza did not know how to say no. By the time she was twenty-three, Eliza had declined three offers of marriage. Her father was proud that Eliza had her own interests and that these did not involve taking part in the humiliating process of falling in love.

Eliza spent days painting fruit and wildflowers in the small kitchen where the morning light sparkled. It became hard to work. Almost every day, the mother of a different eligible son would appear with gifts of cakes, biscuits or fruit to ask Eliza how she spent her Sundays.

'I *paint*,' Eliza would say, finally not even attempting to hide her irritation.

'On the Sabbath?' The women looked shocked.

'Yes. For me, painting is rest. I believe God approves of such things. And I need to paint on the Sabbath because on no other day will people leave me alone.'

When Eliza's father died suddenly and unexpectedly, Eliza grew increasingly angry. She had rebuffed all the eligible young men and could no longer walk in the town without receiving cold glares. It was time for her to leave.

~

I HAVE BEEN wearing a strait-waistcoat in my dreams. If I have managed to remain in bed through the night, I wake in the mornings almost strangled by snakes of Annie's hair around my neck and wrists, smothered by her hand over my face. My wrists are tender and bruised. As soon as I wake, I pull myself free. But Matron does not like us to get up early; she says we should all remain in the one place so that she knows where we are in case anything should go wrong.

During the night I hear voices. Each night they say different things, and when I wake in the mornings I wonder if they were part of my dreams. The voices speak when the berths are blackest and I cannot see whose lips are moving.

'I am not . . . Stay . . . their money . . .'

In the morning while the others sigh in their sleep, I talk to the birds. There are six of them left in a small cage in our berth. Yesterday, one blackbird was discovered, a stiff clump of feathers, on the floor of the cage; this has cast a shadow over the others. They are intended to be a joyful reminder of home to those in the colony but I fear they will not survive the journey. They seem confused and slow in the semi-darkness. For songbirds they are very quiet, with the exception of the other blackbird who has been emitting a high-pitched scream for two days. The scream is growing waves of sound, but its pitch does not alter. Fortunately, the sound can barely be heard over our tin cups and plates clattering together, the creaking ropes and the flapping of the door over the hatchway. If his sound were more piercing I would fear for his life.

I have named the birds. I can only assume Archimedes is grieving for his lost mate and his reduced circumstance. He does not enjoy having to associate with Artemis and Poseidon, the pretty brown-streaked larks. These birds also seem quite unsettled, for they keep stirring up dust and dirt particles from the floor of the cage and trying to work them into their feathers with pointy beaks. Horus the thrush has a swollen and yellow left eye. He is some-what plumper than the other birds and sits in solitary dig-nity on the highest perch. Lares and Penates are more youthful and dance between perches when the mood takes them.

As I was climbing back into bed this morning after

talking to the birds, the girl in the top bunk above our bed saw me. I noticed her glazed eyes behind a frail curtain of hair. I do not know her name. I have not heard her say a word to anyone this whole journey; not even Matron or Eliza attempt to communicate with her. During the day this girl lies with her eyes closed, curled up and facing the wall. She does not have to share a bed. The girl did not weep with Annie or Eliza, nor did she plan and chatter with Beth and Charlotte, when we first arrived. She is the only one of us who is permitted to keep her trunk in the berth. As far as I know, no one has dared ask her why. The trunk is rough and cumbersome; I am certain that I am not the only one who has torn stockings on its corners. I wonder if she is perhaps not going all the way to New Holland but is alighting en route. However, I have not heard that the vessel will be stopping elsewhere. I have not seen her open the trunk and have become curious as to its contents. It is possible that it is filled with books, which would do much to relieve the monotony of this voyage.

Although she had her trunk in the berth, the girl was the first to pack her other belongings into the two canvas bags they gave us. She hung the canvas bags over her bedpost, wrapped herself in a shawl and climbed trembling up to her bed. She has not moved from there since except to use the water closet. She is quite plump and her cheeks are pink with warmth. This morning I did not know what to say to her. I was frightened to speak in case I woke the others. I wondered if it had been her voice that spoke during the night. I was frightened to ask a question that would not be answered.

⌒

MY ONCE WATERTIGHT skin is leaking. It is cold and sticky as salt pork and as taut as canvas. I am dusted with hair the lightness of pollen. I ooze different colours and am grateful for the warm core of blood inside me, though even that has turned from rich scarlet to clumps of brown.

My bones have not yet taken on what Mother called the shape of a woman. During the night when I know that Annie sleeps, I measure the width of my hip bones with my fingers to see if I have grown wider. Mother always said that when I first learn to love, I will become a woman. She said I will know true love by the swelling of my thighs and the expanding of my hip bones. My body will develop pulses in all sorts of new places. Sometimes I fear that I will never love a man as a husband and that my body will remain as slight and flat as it is now. I wonder if my journeys as well as my love will be marked in rings upon my bones.

There is no longer enough water within me to weep. Perhaps the moon has drawn the liquid from my eyes and drops of me are keeping the vessel afloat. I believe the ocean has been collecting the tears of women and sailors for centuries. She takes lives to replenish her waters and she savours the tears of the drowned.

I no longer know my destination. I hope that it is not underneath the weight of blue ocean. I fear that we will catch alight, that the vessel will glow brilliantly and sink like the sun into the sea. No one will know our final resting place. Our bones and charred skin will float together in the black water; merging, sticking, fusing into each other. We will be swallowed, a single mass, by gaping fish.

I must confess that, more than Father, Mother, William and Polly, I think of Richard. I cannot be more than a day without seeing his face in my mind. He grins and I can see the gap between his two front teeth, big enough to trap my little finger. I long to laugh at him, to say, 'Be off with you, Richard,' but when I reach out to touch him he is not there. These visitations frighten me, for I do not really know what he is doing. Whether he is looking after himself, whether he is healthy and keeping in the spirit of things. It is easier not to remember, to pretend that my circumstances now are not connected in any way with his existence.

North of Canary Islands
July 13, 1854

2. Mrs Louisa Garnett
c/- Frederick Garnett, Esq.
'Farraways'
Dorrington
Shropshire

My dear Mother,
　　　　I remember . . .

THE WARMER WEATHER is tightening my skin and bathing in salt makes me look like a plucked chicken. I am being altered by the sea. All the time I am changing. My sense of self is changed by the temperature of the ocean. Thoughts flow with more fluidity than they did in Shropshire. I can no longer wall them in.

Eliza has been asking me about the bruises and cuts on my skin. I could only tell her that my arms have been weakened because I no longer play music. Doctor Carpenter has given me a mustard poultice to draw the infection from my left hand, which still oozes from the knife wound. He smeared table mustard on linen and warmed it before the fire in the galleys. The smell of cooking mustard seed made me hungry. I am not to be captain of our mess again until I have healed. The doctor inspects the wound each morning.

'You are of the sea, Sarah,' he says. 'The red sea,' he chuckles. 'Millions of tiny creatures swim around in your bloodstream, pumped by the current of your heart.' Whenever I prick my finger with a needle, I notice that my blood is becoming a deeper red from all the salt. If I peeled back my skin, I wonder if I, too, would have strands of slimy seaweed lining my shores.

I wonder if Doctor Carpenter knows about the growing fish in my belly. That sometimes it chews the inside of my skin, and that it swallows most of my food. He arrives just before breakfast and bandages my fingers with a grey rag. I want to ask him where he found the rag; I long to know what it was used for, before it became tied around my fingers. The first time he applied the mustard poultice, all I felt was a burning itch that caused me to tear the bandage from my hand while asleep. In the morning I awoke to find the sheets streaked rusty brown. When Annie discovered the blood stains on her cotton nightdress she went into hysterics for several minutes before Eliza could calm her. We told Doctor Carpenter about Annie's turn, and he said we were to keep an eye on her. He said that if Annie displayed this behaviour again, she would need to be given iron pills. It is very important she pays attention to the regularity of her bowels.

Doctor Carpenter wraps the rag so tightly that I lose the sensation in my hand. He says this way my hand will heal with less discomfort. Matron stands near him while he attends to me. He finishes around the same time as Mr Greenwood appears with our breakfast, a large saucepan full of brose. This is a strange Scottish dish that is unnatural to the English appetite. I am acquiring a taste for it, however. Dislodging grains from between my teeth is proving an adequate pastime.

Every morning Doctor Carpenter peers into the saucepan and says, 'Let me see what they are feeding our young ladies for breakfast,' before helping himself to a large bowlful. It is the third morning running that he has swallowed more than a whole portion of our food. We all go hungry when Doctor Carpenter pays a visit.

~

AFTER RICHARD CAME to live with us, Mother allowed me out into the garden to play with the boys. She made them stand before her as she granted them permission to take me outside.

'Look after her,' she said sternly. 'Make sure that Sarah remains warm and dry.'

In those early years, there was much freedom. Richard and William would take me with them to play by the Severn. The first time William splashed me, I screamed and squeezed my eyes shut. It was only after several minutes of Richard's coaxing that I opened them again.

~

THE PITCH OF the ocean slapping the vessel is dropping now as we reach even higher seas. This is of some comfort, because it means we are well on our way to the New World. But I know that increased depth means increased danger. It means that in addition to the freezing water-temperatures we would have to endure if the vessel were to sink, we would also have to attempt keeping ourselves afloat in even greater depths. There is much ocean to swallow us from view.

The tiny ocean at my feet is growing. Each day the spray leaves its mark higher and higher up the walls. I have come to realise that the vessel is not the solid home upon the ocean we have been led to believe. Our direction is determined only by a skeleton of tangled ropes and the angles of canvas. Yesterday one of the main sheet sails was blown right off the ship and into the water. A sailor dived after it and wrapped it around himself to carry it back on board. But as the sailor climbed the ladder, the sheet caught on a nail and was torn. The captain is very angry. We are already running out of spare sails and it is not possible to repair torn sails to their former state, for the repair process always causes more holes which allow the air through.

Every day the vessel becomes more fragile; the snap of a mast would cause her to limp all the way to the New World. We smell the remains of a thousand cargoes browned beyond recognition and seeping into the pores of her wood. Beneath us, she is slowly rotting. I heard that the captain yesterday sent a sailor down to inspect her below the pump wells. He had seen foul smoke rising and had become alarmed that the vessel was on fire. Sometimes we hear the snapping of her joints like a pistol shot.

We have brought our boxes up for the first time. There were shrieks of excitement as we all rediscovered objects that had been missed or forgotten. Matron says we must be prepared for great changes in weather and that we should put aside clothes for great warmth and extreme cold.

'Your clothes may save you, garls,' she muttered several times, before we allowed our boxes to be taken away once more.

Matron said that a beautiful servant girl had travelled on her last voyage. Alice had bones as fine as a bird's and long, pointed toes. She could never keep still. She was always dancing quick steps up and down the monkey poop. The sailors would hang from the rigging and cheer. She reminded them of their duties, they claimed: they knew that they needed to steer the ship with concentration in order to protect the beautiful dancing girl and prevent her from dancing into the ocean.

Matron had been concerned that one of her unmarried women should be an object viewed shamelessly by so many men. She often asked Alice to sit still. Alice knew how to sit quietly on a wooden bench holding her back straight, but she could not stop her feet from prancing around in front of her. It was as though her feet were separate from the rest of her body. Although Alice did not complain when she was ordered to sit still, her eyes dripped large drops of liquid salt to the boards. When she did not dance, the sailors grew lethargic and spent too long staring into the water. They became mesmerised by the sea. In the end, even the captain was losing concentration. He feared the ship would run aground.

One evening, the captain asked Matron to allow Alice to dance. 'She flutters like a butterfly,' the captain said, 'and is necessary for our safe voyage.' So Alice was permitted to dance on the poop and was allowed in all sections of the vessel, even those where other girls were not permitted. The girl went to many areas of the ship where Matron could no longer watch her. The sailors and the captain guided the ship with their original vigour. The breeze fluttered with light and laughter.

One day the girl was spinning on the deck in a crimson gown holding the end of a long red shawl. Her hair fell loose and twisted around her and she spun faster and faster, and higher off the deck. She did not notice that no one was watching her. She did not realise she was alone on deck in near darkness. She spun up with the sea breeze and landed softly in the water. In the water the girl continued to spin for several moments. Then she realised that the sea air was being drawn into her lungs and that it was no longer air, but liquid salt, glowing faintly in the moonlight.

When the girl surfaced, she became alarmed that the ship would sail on without her and that she would be left there to drown, alone in her crimson gown that the captain had given her, with no one to see her spin to the bottom of the sea. Then she felt a miracle occurring. One end of the shawl was caught on the cable-holder at the stern, from which the bower anchors were slung. The other end remained pinned to her breast. Rather than anchor the vessel, the girl was being drawn along behind.

Because she had swallowed so much air, the girl was light and the shawl did not tear. She spent a whole night trailing behind the vessel, her legs kicking in the water so that she felt that she was propelling the vessel and without her dancing they would be held in place.

When the sun rose in the morning, the girl began to call up into the sky. By this time she was stiff with cold and she prayed that no one would see her legs growing swollen in the water.

Eventually the girl heard the cries of a sailor who had noticed that she was missing. When he peered overboard she tried to smile and to flick strands of wet hair behind her head, but her hair fanned and floated with a will of its own. The sailor unhooked the scarf from the cable-holder and pulled. The girl willed her legs to life and used them to climb the exterior of the boat, while reaching up her hands for him to take.

By the time the girl reached the poop, several sailors were on deck to cheer. The sailor who had helped her set her down and she began to spin. She sprinkled the sailors while they cheered. She spun herself dry.

The first thing I saw when I opened my box was Grandmother Fryer's hair. It was coiled as neatly as if I had packed it myself, as stiff as if it had never been wet. How strange to see the chemise, sheets, body jacket and coverlet exactly the way I folded them before I left home. The air from Shropshire had been folded into the creases and I was sad to release it into the staleness of the vessel. I held my stiff handkerchief over my face and breathed in Shropshire as though I could go back there. I could almost smell the sweetness of Richard's breath captured in the linen. I tried to remember when I had last felt his warmth. When I opened my eyes I saw that all the black fabrics were spotted with mould and my red stockings had tinted a pair of stays pink.

Charlotte screamed on opening her trunk. There was a flattened mouse underneath a jar of jam, its innards turning green on her lace petticoat.

Under the top layer of clothing I discovered a pair of drawers which belong to my mother. I wonder if she has noticed they are gone. I see her peering into the cupboard and frowning in the way that makes her chin look lopsided. I watch her as she counts the drawers folded neatly in a soft pile. I see the frown dissolve into laughter as I tell her that Florrie has given me her drawers.

'If only Florrie would give me *your* drawers by mistake,' she says.

My mother's drawers are twice the width of my waist. Now they are the only remembrance of my mother that I have. They have been scrubbed thin and yellow. The waist sags and even after being flattened in my trunk they fill with air and take on her shape. I am sure they are clean and that Florrie did not mean to put them in my cupboard, yet they hold the scent of Mother's rose water as though she has only just removed them.

⁓

ROSE WATER WAS the only liquid Mother could bear. While Mother had always been wary of liquid, it was not until Polly was born that her fear deepened. She remained indoors at the slightest hint of cloud. The ocean appeared in her nightmares. She rushed past rivers and lakes without looking at them. When it rained, she would go to bed and pull the covers over her head. Water could do much damage, she said. It could swell ceilings and make roofs collapse. It could cause people to drown or catch pneumonia. In its natural state it could not help but make people cold. There was altogether far too much of it around, she said. It encouraged mould and rising damp. She feared it would seep into every part of our lives.

Her skin and eyes became dull, her fingernails so brittle that they would snap at the slightest movement. Her hair, although she wore it in a loose bun, soon fell out in thin strands, which trailed around the house.

She came to use the water closet once a day, in the morning, and I knew from the tautness of the muscles in her face whether or not the ritual was over.

Mother particularly despised perspiration and blood. The human body was meant to be as dry as dust, she said, or we would have been creatures of the deep. She carried several handkerchiefs with her at all times to blot the excess fluid from her skin. Mother believed that people who consumed vast amounts of water had more accidents. Their bodies were more clumsy, they were more inclined to indulge in reckless behaviour. They experienced more physical pain through cuts and gashes that allowed some of the liquid out. Bleeding was the body's method of trying to rid itself of the liquid that had managed to find its way in. Infection and vomiting were clear signs of indulging in too much fluid.

Mother turned a blind eye to Florrie's cleaning. She pretended not to be aware that Florrie used buckets of water and soap to mop the floors and to wipe the kitchen table. She did not think about the hot water that filled the copper in the laundry and the way our clothes would occasionally be steamed clean and wrung dry. For, even more than moisture, Mother abhorred dirt.

~~~~~~~

TWO DAYS AGO was cleaning day. We had to air our mattresses on deck and scrub our floorboards thoroughly. All the time, Annie sat sulking at the dining table because the pig had found its way into her bag and eaten her cheese. We were all quite relieved because, although we would not have dared say so, the cheese was going bad and our entire mess was beginning to smell of it.

I pulled off our grey sheet and lifted the mattress. The Donkey Breakfast Mattress is as flimsy as a sack and now it has a small, red-rimmed hole in the middle. Shreds of drowned women's clothing are scattering the berth. As well as bolsters and blankets, metal plates and cutlery, these mattresses that were issued to us on arrival were supposed to be new. However, I cannot recall any incident which could have caused the hole. It looks as if a rat has chewed through to the other side. Although I did not require assistance, Eliza took two corners while I took the other two. We stumbled, laughing, up the uneven stairs to the deck. At times it was only the mattress linked to Eliza which stopped me tumbling back down to steerage. There is no sensation quite like emerging from the musty grey beneath the decks into brilliant sunlight and sharp sea air. We shook the dust, the tiny grains of salt and the stale breadcrumbs from the fabric while we moved. Then Eliza and I swung the mattress towards the captain's cabin, where all the other mattresses were already laid out. I returned to finish cleaning.

At home it was always Florrie who did the dirtiest work. Though I am sure she did not have to crawl in puddles amongst rat droppings, pig manure, crumbs of stale bread and shrivelled meat. Although the sea is much calmer now, I made myself ill scrubbing the floor. I wore one of Florrie's old aprons, bless her. I rubbed the seabed of the small ocean with soap. But this did little more than loosen the dirt, which continued to flow in salty, foaming waves along the boards. I can see now, that a ship could be a vessel of death, and how easy it would be for us all to become ill or to meet with disaster.

After cleaning out the berths, all the girls apart from Annie sat sewing their sun bonnets on the monkey poop, a shade-cloth rigged taut above us. Annie was hacking at her toenails with her large rusty scissors below deck. She collects her nail clippings into a pocket-handkerchief, which she hides under her pillow. During the night I sometimes hear her picking strands of meat from between her teeth with corners of toenail.

Whenever I am on deck, I look for Richard. I cannot help looking. He has a way of appearing when least expected. Mother told me once that his father was the same.

On the way to our end of the monkey poop, we walk past women with drawn faces and tangled hair. The schoolmaster stoops over their shoulders one after the other while the women squint at their books and hold them close to their noses. They point at the words with blackened fingertips and do not realise that the books they hold are upside down.

A group of four men from cabin class sit on wooden chairs near the edge of the deck facing the water. They conduct earnest discussions whilst holding taut twine leading into the ocean. At first I thought they were fishing. When I suggested this to Beth, she laughed. Beth has explained to me that the men are corning pork. It is a strictly scientific process, she said. Chunks of raw meat are tied solidly in twine and hung overboard to a particular depth for a specific length of time. If the pork is hung for too long or too deep, the fibres of meat will be so infused with salt that they will become inedible. Sometimes the twine is tied to the railing. However, it is safest to keep a close eye on the twine. Although there is always a danger that fish or even sharks will discover the bait, salt water is the best possible solution for corning meat. Meat that has been corned in this way may be preserved for years after it is exposed to fresh air.

Matron said we should not be too particular about the appearances of our bonnets. She said it was of utmost importance that we would be able to use them as soon as possible so that we would not die of sunstroke.

Suddenly, a rough hand punched my arm. 'How could you do such a thing?' Annie had come up. Her face was swollen and spotted with tears. She dragged me by the hair over to the edge of the deck. Our mattress with its red-rimmed hole was sinking rapidly beneath the waves. 'Mattress on the port bow!' shouted one of the sailors from above. But I could not help thinking at once of the antiseptic properties of sea water, and that if our mattress were to be rescued, we could at least be sure of its cleanliness.

One by one, the girls left their bonnets and ran to view the spectacle. The giggling attracted the attention of Matron, who started calling out in alarm, 'Garls, garls, go back to your seats!' She waddled red-faced towards us and peered into the water.

'Who is responsible for this?' Even Annie fell silent. Matron began to pace the deck with small steps.

'Those mattresses, like the rest of your belongings, were issued to you as precious gifts from the British Government. You are fortunate to be given the opportunity to better yourselves in a new land. Providence may or may not carry you there. Kneel!' We lowered ourselves to the deck. I folded my skirts behind my knees and tried not to think about how stained they would soon become. I bowed my head and closed my eyes.

'Almighty God, Father of our Lord Jesus Christ, Maker of all things, Judge of all men; We acknowledge and bewail our manifold sins and wickedness . . . We do earnestly repent, And be heartily sorry for these our mis-doings . . .' Matron gasped for breath. 'Amen.'

I opened my eyes. A puff of wind began to stir the sun hats. A bonnet embroidered with small blue forget-me-nots scuttled along the deck. Eliza clasped her hands together and forced her eyes back to Matron's swollen face. One by one we were all beginning to wilt under the sun. All of a sudden, Charlotte's red-bowed hat was swept up from her abandoned chair and circled delicately above us, before dropping to the sea.

'Unless one of you accepts responsibility for this child-ish act,' Matron threatened, 'you will all be confined to steerage for two days!'

'Excuse us, ladies.' Before Matron had further opportu-nity to speak, two sailors had dived over the deck and were swimming towards the mattress. One man collected the bonnet and placed it on his head, where it remained as he dragged our mattress through the water.

Matron stood aghast while we watched the two sailors, their white suits billowing under water. The men, kicking hard, were trying to pull the mattress to the vessel in spite of the choppy waves. Although the ship was not moving quickly, the sailors could not keep up. It was several min-utes before they were close enough to the vessel for another sailor to throw a rope into the water. One sailor tried to hold our mattress while the other pulled the rope through the hole and tied a large knot.

The mattress dangled alongside, slapping the vessel like

a wet rag while the two sailors bobbed up and down in the water.

'Come on, Colier!' one of them shouted.

The mattress flapped towards deck.

A rope studded with large knots was thrown down to the sailors. They laughed and joked and dangled. A sailor crawled across the deck pretending to reach out his arms to Beth. Matron ushered us away.

Many of the sailors have tattoos on their arms. I asked Beth about tattoos and she says they are caused by sharp knives and coloured blood. The body makes pictures of its own, she says, when one attempts to carve it with a knife. She says she has heard that the sailors lie on the poop when everyone else has gone to bed. They drink large amounts of gin, which they steal from the boxes belonging to the cabin passengers. After the gin, the sailors work in pairs; one sailor will lie naked on his chest while the other sits fully clothed on the first man's back. The clothed man uses his sleeves to mop blood as he punctures the skin on the naked man's arms, singing sea shanties while he works. It can take a long time to create a word or a picture, and you can never be sure of the colour until the dead skin covering the wound has peeled off. Some sailors have ships or anchors. Most have their sweetheart's names or important messages imprinted on their skin. Sly Joe has the phrase, *When this you see, remember me*, in untidy handwriting on his upper arm. Beth could not tell me whether the words were supposed to be a reminder of Sly Joe himself or of the drunken sailor who carved his arm by moonlight.

In the evening, just before the unmarried women had to make their way below deck once more, I saw an albatross. He soared high above us and, as I imagined what we must look like from such a height, I began to laugh. How small our vessel must appear, a speck on the vast ocean. What a game this is—how foolish is the man who believes he may conquer such a powerful force. How do we know, when one wave rises much like another, where we are going, and that we are travelling in the right direction at all? The wind blows us in whichever direction she pleases, the sea tosses to watch us stumble and scald ourselves with cups of tea. The pale sunlight can colour the ocean turquoise while dark clouds shadow her grey.

After everyone had gone to bed in the evening, Annie and I once again sharing our even flatter, salty mattress, I felt that the fish in my belly slept. I stroked it. When I was almost asleep, I remembered the birds. I have not spent so much time with them since the days have been brighter and warmer. I wondered if anyone had remembered to give them fresh water.

The floorboards were wet and grainy under my bare feet. The light above the hatchway created a dim glow, just enough for me to make out the shape of the pig's swollen rear underneath Beth's bed.

The pig now has a bell tied around her neck. She shakes her head in greeting and the soft ringing echoes around steerage. I have seen Matron peer at us all quizzically, trying to discover the source of the sound. It is the only music we hear for days at a time. The ringing is silenced only when the pig sleeps. It was Beth who discovered the bell under her mattress, wedged into the wood of her berth. She said that in medieval times, a bell would be tied around the neck of animals not fit for slaughter. She said we needed to invent a disease for the pig, so that the other passengers would think its flesh was infected and poisonous, and would therefore not want to kill it.

I could see Artemis and Poseidon sitting near each other on the top perch. Horus sat a few inches from them, his eye less swollen now. Lares and Penates were on opposite ends of the lower perch. Suddenly I noticed Archimedes, the other blackbird, stiff on his back with his wiry legs in the air. It must have been the heat that killed him. Or the lack of light. If only I had thought to ask Matron if we could take them on deck with us. If only I had not prayed so hard for warmer weather.

I feared waking the other girls as I reached into my canvas bag to find my prayer book. Inside the cover I discovered the linen handkerchief Polly gave me for my last birthday. *Sarah, 16*, is embroidered in curly red script. Gently I lifted the small doorway to the birdcage while the other birds flapped in alarm. My hands shook as I lifted Archimedes from the floor of the cage and wrapped him in my handkerchief. He would have a formal burial service tomorrow. I hid his cold body under my pillow.

In the dim lamplight, I noticed the quiet girl's unblinking eyes. She reached out to touch my hair. I smiled at her, and climbed under my blanket.

In the early morning I woke once again to the sensation of having heard voices. A girl was crying and saying, 'Knife . . . throat . . .'

The days now are still and sunny. The sky is lighter than I have ever seen it before. I stare up into the heavens, wondering what is hidden behind the blue and where the stars have gone. The soft sunlight makes my eyes water. The sea sparkles and everything is coated in pale lemon haze.

Mr Greenwood said that if we were well behaved, he would take us to see the captain's garden. The captain grows greenery in a box of earth in the jolly-boat. The jolly-boat is hoisted up and stored at the stern of the ship. This provides the garden with some shelter from the elements. Mr Greenwood told us that people have begun eating the captain's produce and that they have never tasted such crisp lettuce or spring onions before. He said that the sea air makes vegetables particularly moist and gives them a more pronounced flavour. It is a long time since I saw leaves that were not limp and withered. And it is difficult to imagine that it is possible to grow plants so far from land. I wish I were permitted to sit near them.

Richard gave me a rose bush for my last birthday. In the morning I would go down to the garden and stroke the deep burgundy petals which opened out like eyelids. Every day that I did not see him, I watered the rose with sweet tea that was left over from breakfast. The petals deepened in colour. The thorns sharpened. Now I long for smooth leaves to cry into.

The ship rocks slowly. The captain tells us we are moving towards the Canary Islands, yet I do not believe we are moving at all. I pray for the north-east trade winds that Mr Greenwood says will carry us towards the Brazils. We are in the Sargasso Sea, which is thick with gulf weed. If I squint, I am surrounded by fields of uninterrupted soft grass. I feel that I am nowhere.

I have heard that we are at the horse latitudes. I do not know what latitudes these are exactly, but Mr Greenwood tells us that we are nearing the point at which the cargo ships usually begin to run out of fresh water. I laughed when Mr Greenwood said the word *fresh* for I have rarely known the water on board to be anything other than rancid and swimming with life, or salt.

On the day of the last picnic it rained blunt needles as Polly and I were making our way home. We danced under water until our dresses were damp almost to invisibility. We opened our mouths and tilted our heads up to the heavens, swallowing small sharp droplets. That water was fresh. But I know that the water hidden in barrels on this vessel is swarming with creatures. That is why we pour vinegar or raspberry wine into the water before drinking it.

Mr Greenwood looks about our mess and says that because we are nearing the horse latitudes and the vessel holds only one horse, some of us will have to be thrown overboard. There is not enough water for us all, he says. He looks at Annie when he says this and she sniffs, pointing her nose towards the hatchway.

There was once a sailor on a cargo ship who formed a particular attachment to the horses, which were on their way to the Americas. The sailor spent the early hours of every morning in the darkness below the deck singing and stroking the necks of the animals, who had dull, tired eyes. The animals were weak from lack of movement and they grew thin. Their coats were matted. Every now and then one would lie on the dusty floor and die.

The sailor tried to keep them alive. He took them his own molasses and some of his provision of water. He was as thin and dusty as the horses. The vessel was nearing the horse latitudes when the captain became aware that they were running out of supplies. One of the other sailors realised that McGovern was gone from his hammock every morning between the hours of two and three. The other sailor followed him, and told the captain the following morning that McGovern was stealing the provisions.

The captain whipped McGovern until he lay bleeding on the deck. The next morning the captain said that four of the five horses would have to go or the entire crew would perish on the ocean from lack of liquid.

The other sailors stood on the poop and hung from the rigging, cheering while McGovern emerged with a brown gelding which stumbled on the narrow stairs and blinked in the light. The horse flicked its tail and tossed its head. It lifted its feet delicately on the deck. McGovern clamped his jaw while he led the animal to the gangplank. The horse stood at the edge of the deck and held its feet firmly in place. It peered at the waves. McGovern stepped onto the plank, pulled the rope around the horse's neck and clicked his tongue. The animal lifted first one foreleg and then the other until it was standing on the gangplank. The sailor jumped back to the poop and nudged the animal from behind. The horse shrieked as it slipped into the sea.

McGovern could only do this once. The second time he emerged from the hatchway, he wept openly as the white mare followed him. Before anyone could stop him, McGovern jumped onto the animal's dusty back, nudged its side with his heels, and rode the horse into the ocean.

It was several minutes before the sailors realised that McGovern was not going to re-emerge from the sea. 'Man overboard!' one of them had shouted from the rigging. He laughed. But then he saw that some of the others were already throwing ropes into the water.

The sailors tied their ropes to the masts. Some dived overboard. They opened their eyes in the green water. Some claimed they saw McGovern riding the white mare beneath the ocean. She tossed her head, they said, and seemed free at last. He was sitting astride her. He stroked her neck and whispered into her ear. McGovern's body was never found.

Whenever I am on the poop, I stare into the sea, which contains the bodies of so many horses. I look for McGovern. I want him to tell me stories about life under the waves. I want to ride the brown gelding beside him under the sea. Yesterday I saw an old sailor's cap floating beneath the water. It was cream-coloured with fading blue. I called out to Beth that I had found McGovern's hat. She opened her eyes very wide and raised her eyebrows.

'You don't believe that story, do you?' she asked.

Charlotte, Eliza and I take turns in keeping watch from the deck. We cannot all watch at once or Matron will notice that we are not working. So two of us stitch while the other holds the canvas up close to her face, peering sideways into the water. We have not decided exactly what we will do when we find him. Though we do hope to give him some molasses for the horses and biscuits, which will become soft after soaking in the sea. We would like him to tell us of his adventures. If it is truly possible to live under water then perhaps we will be safer there. I think of Grandmother Fryer and wonder if I, too, can breathe under water.

Perhaps breathing under water is something that can be learned and taught. I could establish my own colony beneath the waves. Richard and I could build a cottage of coral.

His face is fading from my memory now. I fear that means he is growing weak in spirit.

With Matron's permission, Mr Greenwood took our mess to see the captain's garden. Matron thought there might be seeds and soil somewhere on board and that Mr Greenwood might help us to plant our own vegetables. She liked the idea that the unmarried women could prove useful to the other passengers. Matron did not hear Eliza say that there was enough dirt in our mess to grow potatoes on our beds. I imagined waking up to the smell of earth.

We arrived at the stern of the ship. From there we could see the small jolly-boat, lightly built and rocking slightly above the deck. It was empty.

We had almost begun to doubt the existence of the garden when the captain appeared, carrying the wooden box of green in his arms. He seemed very tidy in his navy blue, which was the colour of the sea on a sunny day. His chest was studded with brass buttons and his thin hair combed neatly to one side. He had been waiting for us to arrive.

I have heard stories about other captains marrying unmarried women on disembarking in the New World. There is a rumour aboard that the captain's wife died two years ago and that he is now is search of another.

'Ladies.' He turned slowly. His eyes ran up and down our bodies like a wet cloth. I shivered.

The garden was even smaller than I had expected. I believe that only a few passengers will ever have the opportunity to taste these vegetables. There are two wilting lettuces and the tufts of perhaps three carrots. The box is about one-third the size of my trunk. With slow deliberation, the captain placed the box at our feet. While we stood around it, he watched our hands very closely to make sure we did not attempt to peal off any of the outer lettuce leaves, or shred the leaves sprouting from the head of the carrots. Then, as if changing his mind, he reached over with caterpillar fingers and tore a lettuce leaf in half. The leaf was limp and stuck to his fingers.

'What is your name?' He stared at Beth. She stared back.

'Beth Porter,' she said.

'Would you like to try my leaves?' He chuckled and reached out his hand to her. She gripped the green between two fingernails and peeled it from his skin. She put it on her tongue and chewed silently.

'Look!' Charlotte exclaimed. 'A cocoon!'

'Surely not.' The captain frowned. 'Where?'

'On the back wall of the box.'

'Ladies, my garden is clean!' A fat brown roll swung from the edge of the wooden box.

Beth leaned over the box and tugged at the roll. She said she could feel it trembling in her fingers.

Four of us leaned over the box and began to blow warm air.

'My garden is well-tended and free of pests.' The captain watched Beth's chest as she began peeling the layers of brown. He grew restless and began pacing. Before long, Beth had freed the new butterfly from its shell. Our last memories of the monarch were carried away by the sea breeze.

⌒

EVEN THE HOUSE suffered from Mother's need for dryness. The wallpaper had not been resealed for a number of years and was beginning to flake. Occasionally when someone entered the house through the front door, sections of plaster would crumble from the ceiling and sprinkle their hair with powder. The mantel above the fireplace in the drawing room featured a huge crack that Mother eyed with satisfaction. Even the house was attempting to rid itself of excess moisture.

Mother hated to wash. She would close her eyes and clasp her arms around her chest once a week while Florrie wiped a flannel over her face. Florrie would have to sing to her while pulling back her clothes and scrubbing her armpits. Mother would shudder and gasp. We would hear her from downstairs.

Mabel was instructed to cook with minimum moisture. Meat and potatoes were nearly always baked. Mother would enjoy them most when overcooked: beef in fat strands with no gravy and potatoes in a crust. But Mabel even had to be careful when overcooking meals because if you overcooked potatoes for too long they turned to mush. I learned to swallow flavourless food in small quantities.

Mother said that not enough was known of the properties of water for us to be sure of its goodness. When I was eight years old, she announced she would no longer be drinking liquids of any sort. Mabel stared in horror from behind but said nothing. Father continued to saw at his mutton. Polly swallowed and traced the flowers on the tablecloth with her eyes.

'Naturally I cannot stop you from drinking,' Mother whispered in her husky voice. 'But I certainly cannot recommend it. Water contains hundreds of life forms and we cannot be sure they will not harm us.'

Mabel grew nervous and her hands trembled with such vigour that she had trouble serving the meal. As she walked towards the table, she lost her grip on a jug of water and it slipped in her grasp. She caught the jug only after tipping its contents on the floorboards. Mother shrieked.

'Calm!' Father ordered. Mabel had slipped then and landed on her back, thumping her head on the floor while the jug rolled away from her. Mother began to choke with dry, rasping sobs.

'Sarah,' Father said quietly. 'Lay your hands on Mabel's temples and put a finger before her mouth. Does she appear to be breathing?'

'Yes, Father.'

'Good. Now, loosen her clothing. Polly, ask Florrie to find some spirit of sal volatile.'

After Florrie and Father had taken Mabel to her quarters to recover, Mother stood trembling in the corner. She had long ceased speaking to me like a child.

'The water, Sarah . . .' she whispered, pointing at the wet floor. 'A pool . . . a reflection . . .'

The following morning, Mother was not at breakfast.

'She is not feeling well, Miss,' Florrie told me as she poured my tea.

When I entered Mother's room, I saw her lying still as death with eyelids like dry leaves sealing her face. I could feel heat emanating from her body.

Mother was still for two days. We tried to pour water

into her mouth but she refused to part her lips. With the impatience of a child, Polly tried to force them apart. Mother snapped. Florrie held a cold compress to her forehead and Mother tore the wet fabric from her coarse skin.

On the third day, Father called the doctor. Doctor Osbourne conducted a thorough examination while we waited outside the room.

'I can find little wrong with her,' he began, 'but you must try to make her drink. Her body is beginning to shrivel from lack of moisture.'

We began with small cups of warm tea that she drank more readily than cold water. At first she lacked strength to open her eyes. I would tell her of the healing properties of warm tea and lift her up while Polly parted her lips and poured small quantities of sweet liquid into her mouth. Under her chin we could see sharp movements and we knew she was swallowing the drink. That afternoon she opened her eyes and lifted the corners of her mouth into a smile.

'There is nothing wrong with *a little* tea,' she whispered.

I HAVE BECOME accustomed to the movement of the ocean and no longer remember the sensation of walking on land. But I move about so little that any exertion makes my ankles ache. I wish I could climb the ropes. I would be able to see so much more from above. It was Richard who taught me to climb. When we started playing together, he explained that I needed to learn to trust the strength in my limbs. My own body would need to carry me, he said. But these last few weeks my body has been my hindrance. Lack of movement has made me stiff and slow.

As we near the Canary Islands, we are surrounded by flying fish. I have always associated wings with creatures more delicate: butterflies, birds and angels. These fish are silver-grey; they jump from the sea, flapping on deck. I have heard that some of the men are drying fish skins to make journal binding. I cannot imagine that such thin and stiff fabric would not snap at the first use. I could not bear my own words to be carried around like the innards of a rotting fish.

I have noticed that the men will catch anything that moves. It is their primary preoccupation, which is probably why Matron keeps such a strict eye. I think it makes them feel as though they have some power over existence. They like to watch the life drip with the water from the flanks of sea creatures until they are too weak to move. Yesterday the men struggled with a baby shark. We watched from further along the poop where Matron had fallen asleep sitting on the chicken coop, her head slumped on her bosom. The sailors tied a strong rope around the shark's soft belly and tried to heave him up on deck. Some of the sailors sat in the jolly-boat next to the vessel and tried to push the animal from underneath. I had never seen a shark before, and was surprised at its harmless appearance. The shark struggled, it opened and closed its mouth as though longing to cry out. His teeth were small and pointed. He did not look as though he wanted to chew the life from human flesh. He merely wanted to weave his body through the waves.

They laughed when he wriggled and they delighted in pushing their fingers into the smooth flesh. They did not see the beauty in his sharpened fins and curved body. The creature dangled for a few minutes, tossing its head while the rope tightened around its waist. I could see the rope cutting into elastic skin.

Suddenly the rope snapped. The sailor who had been gripping the rope most strongly fell backwards. The shark landed on the open boat and tipped the men into the water. The sailors shouted. They ran around the deck helplessly. The sound of young women screaming awoke Matron, who hustled us below deck.

We tripped on each other's skirts and slipped on the stairs down the hatchway. We were such a confused mass of petticoats and skirts that I forgot who I was during the moments of being pushed down the stairs.

'Wipe your shoes and descend in an orderly fashion!' Matron shouted, shoving us one after the other while attempting to stand on her toes and peer overboard.

Annie climbed into bed and muttered that she had sprained her ankle. The rest of us stood on the stairs, below the hatchway that was now closed, listening to the commotion on deck.

The boards trembled above us while something heavy was dragged towards the cabins. I held my arms around my chest to stop myself from trembling. Behind me a girl began to whimper.

I AM MOST afraid when the men try to catch albatrosses, for I have heard much about the bird's spirit. The albatross carries white magic in its vast wings. But if it is harmed then black magic will drip from the inky feathers rimming the white. For several days an albatross hung stiffly over starboard. Its wings were outstretched and its beak knocked against the ship like a saddlebag against the flanks of a horse.

One afternoon when Matron was peering into the sea, I crept to starboard to examine the creature. Its wings are a dusty cream and its eye is hard and glazed as a large marble. I felt that it could see through my skin. As the wind blew, its wings appeared to flap and I feared that it would try to catch the Severn-fish swimming in my belly. The albatross has a very long and narrow beak that is almost black. It is cracked and appears over-used.

The men bait albatrosses with our shrivelled pork, but, once they catch them, have trouble finding a use for the creatures. The feathers can be plucked and the skins dried. But there is little use for the flesh. I heard that one of them, a Scotsman, tried to make a pie from albatross feet for his mess. He climbed down to steerage with the bird upon his back so that he looked as though he might fly. He laid the beast on the table and took a carving knife to saw through the leathery limbs. He then planted chunks of webbed albatross foot into pastry and took it up to the galleys to bake. He said the feet would make jelly like pigs' trotters. The man thought that using the feet would not be bad luck so long as he did not break the wings. The cook left the galley while the pie baked. When the pastry had browned, the Scotsman carried the dish back down to his mess. The other men went hungry rather than taste the pastry, which smelt so strongly of fish. The man who baked the pie ate it himself in one night. After the first bite he described the sweetness of the flesh and how it tasted like paradise. He has been in the ship hospital ever since, feverish and weak. He has begun to speak in tongues. He has a huge collection of muddy albatross feathers next to his bed and he flies into a rage if anyone tries to take them away. We call him the Albatross Man.

He is said to tell stories of soaring over the ocean. The sky is golden, he says, when one is within it. He says that the rainbow is a magic pathway leading from reality to paradise. He can fly from our world to the next. When Matron was talking to Eliza, Doctor Carpenter whispered to me that the Albatross Man had offered to take the unmarried women to paradise one by one. We can ride on his back, he said. And when we arrive there we will find enough feathers to make wings of our own, allowing us to fly.

The Albatross Man will not eat anything but fish. He prefers them to be alive and dropped to him from above. The sailors say he is capital entertainment to watch. That they merely drop flapping fish to his chest while he lies in

the ship hospital and he will spring to life. He drops to the
boards like a cat and tries to catch the creature between his
teeth. When he has caught it in his mouth, the Albatross
Man shakes the life from the fish before biting off its head.
He closes his eyes and coos as he munches the head. Then
he begins to peel back the scales from the flesh with his
two front teeth.

One night, the Albatross Man stripped himself naked in
the ship hospital while everyone else slept. He tore his
clothes and hid them in a grey bundle at the foot of his
bed. He then crept back to his mess in steerage. Some of
the other Scotsmen from his mess claim to have seen him,
but since he was not doing any harm, they let him be. The
Albatross Man found a jar of treacle on the dining table.
He made his way back to the ship hospital where he
opened the jar and began to smear himself in treacle. He
spread the albatross feathers on the floor of the ship hospital and rolled in them. When Doctor Carpenter discovered
him the next morning, the Albatross Man was laughing
deliriously, feathers sticking out from his body at all
angles. He was glued to the floor. Doctor Carpenter had to
send the sailors below deck with buckets of sea water
before they could prise him from the boards.

⌒

FOR ONE YEAR after Mother's turn I became slow due
to lack of moisture. I, too, had come to fear the evil effects
of water. I became unused to liquid. I drank little and felt

my blood grow thick. Parchment paper lined my skin inside and I felt warm empty passages of air filling my body. My days were spent with Miss Tucker in the school-room where I read books and did not have to move my limbs. Miss Tucker often said that my eyes were lifeless and I looked old.

My hair was thin and my lips started to flake. In the dark warmth of my room during the night I would peel leaves of skin from my feet. Then I would drop them into the fireplace so that my own ashes contributed to the dryness of the house.

One day it rained and I spent the entire afternoon in the drawing room. I no longer wished to read. Instead, I watched the stream of water flow from the sky. The earth turned black and the leaves bottle green. They were weighed down with water and they swung as the droplets rolled from their tips. I was calmed by the gentle rhythm on the roof.

I kneeled to face the window and clasped my hands over the sofa. My chin rested on the rough skin of my hands. The fire in the hearth warmed and dried my back even further. I watched the rain and began to long for liquid. I ran my dry tongue over shiny teeth and moistened my lips to make them smooth. I wanted to moisten the house.

It was only months before Richard was to arrive.

DURING THE DAY when we are not permitted on the monkey poop, we hear whisperings of many things that are happening around us. There is more bickering in the confined spaces below the poop. On one occasion when we were in steerage, Charlotte asked Beth to return her shawl.

'The white one Harold gave me before he left.'

Beth looked puzzled. 'You didn't show it to me,' she said.

'You asked to borrow it. You said you wanted to wear it to bed to keep you warm,' Charlotte told her.

'No . . . I haven't felt cold.'

'Beth, give it back!'

'I don't have it.'

'You do. You must.' Charlotte's voice was rising in pitch and her cheeks coloured. 'It must be here.' She pulled the blanket off Beth's side of the bed and felt under the rag Beth was using for a pillow.

'How dare you!' Beth pushed Charlotte so that she hit her head on the boards behind the bed. Charlotte's eyes began to water. Beth glared. 'How dare you accuse me of stealing!'

Charlotte began to sob. 'I haven't seen him for two years . . . The shawl is all I have . . . Please, Beth . . .'

Eliza walked over from the dining table and put her arm around Charlotte's shoulders.

'It's all right,' she said. 'We'll find it, Charlotte. It must be somewhere in here.' Beth sat on her mattress and rested her chin in her hands.

EVERY NIGHT I hear the wailing of a child. The mess on one side of us must contain several Irish families. There are so many voices that many family members must share each bed to accommodate them all. As I pulled the sheets over my chest one evening, I heard the Irish woman nearest me through the wood separating us.

'I worry about Ruth.'

'She does not travel well.'

'Her face, it's swollen. She can barely open her eyes.'

'Pray for her, Mary,' the child's father said quietly.

When Mr Greenwood comes to collect our meals after Charlotte has prepared them for baking, he tells us stories about what else is happening on the rest of the vessel. This morning Matron would not let us up on the poop on account of there being an Irishman called Mr Callaghan who has the Blue Devils. Mr Callaghan has been stripping himself naked for all to see. Mr Greenwood says it is capital entertainment because Mr Callaghan is such a good-natured lunatic that he imagines himself to be commander of the ship, and has been giving money to all and sundry. Matron frowned when she heard this, and sent Mr Greenwood away to bake our greengage tart.

There is to be a singing competition on board, with a separate prize for the best male and female singer. We only sing on Sundays and many of us are out of practice, so today our mess began to rehearse. At first Eliza tried to give a starting pitch, but it was flat. She has a strong singing voice, but only plays the pianoforte and is not accustomed to tuning an instrument. If I close my eyes and hold out my left hand, as though holding my violin, I can pitch a concert-A in my head. I can see Polly at the pianoforte on a Sunday evening wearing her silk gown and patiently striking an A while I tune my strings. Now we are ready to play and I can sing my starting note. While he lived with us Richard was often present at our Sunday evening recitals. I would have to concentrate very hard on the music to make sure I did not lose my place.

Sitting on our beds this afternoon, we sang all the major scales starting with A and rising by a semitone each time. We then began arpeggios, and Matron came to complain that we were giving her a headache. It was only when we paused in our practice that we noticed the birds in their cage singing soaring tunes. I had not heard them sing in such a manner during the voyage. Perhaps our music reminds them of other birds, and they have come to life again.

I was pleased to see that even the quiet girl sang with us. She has a sweet voice and sings with confident vibrato. Singing with her made me feel as though I knew her. So much warmth floated down from the top bunk where she sat, that I knew we would be firm friends. I began to climb the ladder to the top bunk where she sat with a blanket over her legs and a shawl over her shoulders.

The girl smiled while the soft sounds flowed from her. During an interval, she told me that her name was Lydia. Her mother had taught her music and she used to sing with her sisters. Lydia said that one day she would like to teach her own child English folksongs. She seemed much older than I. I could not imagine myself to be a mother.

'I would like to have a daughter. Only one, and I would pray for her to be healthy. I would like to go to the grave having passed on everything I have ever seen. This voyage is deep. It makes me so tired. I think I will only be able to tell the story of this voyage once.'

At lunchtime when Mr Greenwood returned with our greengage tart, he told us that Mr Callaghan had become angry that so many fellow passengers were taking advantage of his generosity. He began running from one end of the deck to the other, slashing a horsewhip through the air. The captain caught him and held down his arms, while the first mate pulled a strait-waistcoat over him. Even then Mr Callaghan would not stop shouting and thrashing his arms about. The captain was forced to subdue him with the horsewhip and a large dose of laudanum. Although Mr Callaghan is now safely locked in a cabin, Matron was so alarmed when she heard this story that she grew faint and had to lie down. Doctor Carpenter gave her a compress and some port wine.

Lydia and I planned a midnight feast. We are not permitted on the deck to watch the sunset in the evenings and are sent to bed soon after dinner. It was strange lying in bed and trying to keep from sleeping. I find now that the rocking of the vessel sends me to sleep almost immediately. I lay with my eyes open, trying to remember the words to 'Slap-bang, here we go again' for the singing competition. It was a song Mother would not have liked. I had heard groups of girls from another mess singing it during the day. They clapped as they sang and their words made me laugh.

Beds around me creaked and bodies thumped, trying to settle for the night. When it was quiet, I climbed out of bed and collected my biscuit bag. Lydia helped me onto her bunk in the dark, and brought out some treacle in a pickle bottle.

Just as I was climbing up to Lydia, I heard the voice again.

'. . . any more . . . hide . . . upset Mama . . .'

I peered into Lydia's face. It did not move.

'It's Annie,' she whispered.

Suddenly another body rose from a bunk. I could see from the curly hair that it was Beth and thought at first that she was sleepwalking. She made her way carefully around the shadow of the pig lying near the dining table. I moved to follow her but Lydia touched my hand and shook her head. Beth moved with ghostly steps to the left, towards Matron's cabin. A few minutes later she passed us again, walking quietly past us with the hatchway key in her hand.

Now that Mr Callaghan's rampaging is over, we are permitted on deck once more. Today the ocean barely ripples, and in her depths I see brilliant fires. There is a burning trail and if I could walk on water, I wonder where I would go. This morning as I squinted, trying to see the end of the trail, I began to whisper a chant for the north-east trade winds. There is a rancid smell floating up from the sea. I am grieved to report that Horus is dead.

Doctor Carpenter told us of an extraordinary vision that occurred during the darkness: the ocean became a glimmering blanket of white. The captain and crew were alarmed by the light from beneath the water. The sky was as black as the Earl of Hell's riding boots and the stars shone feebly as though they might soon be extinguished. The captain cast the lead and discovered that there was no bottom at sixty fathoms. They wondered if they had reached a point on the earth where the water travels through the centre. Then they decided to collect a portion of water and examine it more closely. By the light of a lamp, they saw that the water swarmed with sea insects. Doctor Carpenter felt them with his hands. He had never touched such a smooth, cool consistency. He pulled one of the long narrow creatures out with two fingers. It slithered like jelly. When he held it up to the lamp it singed like hair, turned the colour of blood and made a satisfying popping sound, its liquids splattering the table like cooking fat. Many of the creatures formed rings with a row like fine teeth in the centre. The captain and best mate took great pleasure in lifting the animals from the water and holding them up to the lamp, watching them expand and then explode in the heat. But as the sky grew darker and the sea whiter, even Doctor Carpenter became alarmed. He begged the other three men to stop killing the creatures, for there was a new heaviness in the air and he felt God's presence.

They hurried up to the poop and fell upon their knees. They feared it was the end of the world. The best mate stumbled back to the captain's cabin to find the bucket containing the remaining sea insects glowing white. He hurried to the edge of the deck. In his rush to throw the creatures overboard, he dropped the entire bucket into the ocean.

The three men knelt for several hours on the poop with their eyes closed. They muttered prayers of salvation to the dark heavens. Doctor Carpenter was the first one who dared open his eyes. He blinked a number of times. He realised that the sea had returned to its inky colour and the moon was lighting a faint path before them. If it were not for the small lumps of jelly glued to the map in the captain's cabin, they could have dreamed the entire occurrence.

⌒

BELOW DECK I am haunted by the Irish family next to us. I have never seen them but their voices, growing more and more anxious, push through the wall. I had become so accustomed to the child wailing that I am alarmed because now she is nearly silent. It is the mother who sobs now, begging her husband to ask the doctor for more wine and preserved cabbage.

I think of my own father. He spent his days working in the cellar and we were rarely permitted to visit him there. I only remember one occasion of being allowed to descend the stairs. It was not long before Richard came to live with us. I was ten. Father showed me a drop of water under one of his most powerful microscopes. I saw tiny cells wriggling with life. He usually worked with more powerful chemicals and Mother feared that inhaling them would make us ill. She was even more concerned that the moisture from his experiments would seep up through the walls into the house. Ever since her turn, Mother often said that Father was moist by nature. Dryness did not come naturally.

It was through her insistence that he came to spend the evenings in his library with his books. Once there, though, Father seemed to enjoy it. William, whenever he was at home, played chess and drank whisky there. In Mother's presence, Father said that his library was the most comfortable room in the house. Paper blotted the moist atoms that floated in the air.

'The climate is well-moderated by books,' he told us all, smiling to himself. 'It is rarely too damp in a place containing so many leaves.'

For Mother's sake, my father was also careful not to allow himself to become too moist. The skin on his face, whenever I looked at it closely, was peeling from dryness. Flakes of scalp scattered every time he shook his head.

One night I lay in bed next to the window. Gusts of wind flung droplets of water at the glass. Icy air pushed through the cracks in the wood. No matter which way I turned, or how many blankets I used, I could not warm my body. I thought suddenly of Father's library, its embers and its dryness. Clutching two woollen blankets and a pillow, I made my way downstairs.

There was comfort in the smell of paper and worn leather binding. I lit the oil lamp and held my stiff fingers over its flame. I found a small log of wood near the hearth and placed it over the faintly smoking embers in the fireplace. One by one I began to pull books like bricks from the shelves. Trying not to let them thump too loudly, I laid the books in a rectangle next to the hearth. I then covered the books with one of the blankets, pulled the other over my head, and slept.

I was pressed against the pages like a story. I could feel the leather sucking the moisture from my skin, while I became lightly smoked by the fire. In the morning I felt my soul dragged down into the dryness from my sea dreams. I was sure that my body had been robbed of all its fluids. The dryness extended from my bowels to my throat. I lay stiff and still in the heat.

It was not until Mother whipped the blanket from my head that I became fully alert.

'What were you thinking of?' she screamed. 'Ruining your father's books! We thought you had gone out into the water and been struck by the storm.'

FOR SOME TIME now it has been raining sea blood. At first it was thin and almost orange, falling with the dew and splattering the shrouds. Now it is becoming deeper and streaking the decks crimson. Even the tiny ocean lapping at our feet is growing darker. Cranky Jim says it is a bad omen. That we are heading for certain death. The captain laughs and says it is raining desert dust from Africa. Doctor Carpenter says that desert dust, when examined under a microscope, is made up of tiny creatures with very sharp claws and that the crimson on our skin is our own blood.

Whenever we make our way below deck in the evenings, we glow like Christmas lanterns. Salt water makes the red stick to us. There is not enough fresh water to waste on cleanliness. We scrub each other with old rags, which are now almost as crimson as our skin. It is impossible to be clean.

The effort of forgetting when there is so much to remember makes me feel that this is a journey I can only make once. I cannot bear the thought that I have erred.

The Doldrum Calms
August 3, 1854

3. Mrs Louisa Garnett
c/- Frederick Garnett, Esq.
'Farraways'
Dorrington
Shropshire

My dear Mother,
　　　I have stopped . . .

WE ARE IN the Doldrums. Matron has been forced to allow us on deck more frequently as she herself cannot bear the heat below. People fall like rotten trees, collapsing on the boards while others whisper, 'White Man's Grave'. My feet are as ripe as the swollen fruits of the Caribbean. If I could peel them, I would taste sweet flesh.

I feel as though we have been washed into someone's painting. There is no wind in the sails, everything appears frozen in place. There is another vessel shimmering in the distance. She looks like a ghost ship. The air is oppressively hot and brimming with moisture. It clings to my arms like fat fingers. If it would rain, the water would drip from the sky and not linger. It would bring relief. The sea is like glass and I long to step upon it and walk away. We have stopped moving altogether.

One of the sailors yesterday realised that the jib-boom was beginning to sag. On closer inspection it was discovered that this pointed piece of wood that spurs us along and supports much of the rigging has rotted inside. The ship's carpenter has been trying to repair it. He straddles wooden planks and weaves his fingers between oiled ropes. His hammer is the only sound to break the silence. The sailors watch him without speaking, fearing that he will topple overboard and that we will be left without a jib-boom to continue the journey, with nothing to hold the sails and capture the wind that would carry us to the New World.

IT WAS RICHARD who taught me not to be afraid of water. He took my hand and led me quietly to the river while William climbed a tree near the water's edge. He did not say anything, but bent down and pulled me into a squatting position. He pointed the fingers of his free hand and dipped them in the bubbling water. I followed him like a delayed shadow. He drew a line on my forehead with his forefinger. I giggled and flicked droplets in his face.

He led me back up the hillock and sat down in the grass.

'Your boots are getting wet,' he said. 'You had best take them off.'

I pulled the stockings from my ankles and untied my boots. In bare feet I stood, then began to run madly towards the water. Richard shouted something and ran after me. I loved the wind in my hair and the moist grass under my feet. I heard panting and stifled laughter.

'I've caught you!' Richard did not jeer triumphantly as

William did. Instead, he put his arms around me and, laughing, we tumbled to the grass.

~

DURING THE NIGHT I heard whispering from our Irish neighbours.

'. . . commit her to the deep before they find out . . .'

I could not hear the infant but an adult sobbed quietly while footsteps climbed the hatchway stairs.

My face is covered in lumps that sting when I touch them and explode in my sleep. In the mornings I wash the crusts of milky liquid from my hands with sea water.

In the morning there are large red welts and grains of mud on my neck. Eliza says they look like snake bites but Doctor Carpenter is not alarmed. He says they are not infected and that they will not cause any harm. He tells me to keep them clean. He does not know where they come from.

I asked Annie one morning whether they were still noticeable. She smirked. 'Your nightdress is torn! You'll have to mend that or Matron will see. You've been up to no good, haven't you?'

As I dressed, I noticed that my chest was slightly bruised. I found a needle and thread in one of my bags. Frightened that Matron would discover me and ask how I had torn my nightclothes, I sat on my bed in near darkness trying to sew up the tear along the neckline. Eliza touched my arm. 'What are you doing hiding under here?' she asked. When I told her, she shook her head. 'You'll have to watch that Annie.'

Some time ago Eliza started unravelling the bandages from my hand each morning after breakfast. She says Doctor Carpenter will kill me if I trust him to cure my hand, and that the thick moisture must be allowed to dry if I am to regain the use of my fingers. Eliza speculates that perhaps a yeast poultice would be more effective than mustard. She says yeast is a stronger antiseptic and stimulant. She thinks it would make my hand heal faster as it removes dead tissue. We sit together on her bed as she bathes my hand in salt and then tells me to look away when she squeezes the wound. 'I must draw out the infection, Sarah,' she tells me as I clamp my jaw together. 'Please be brave.' My hand is returning to its usual size and Doctor Carpenter is pleased. He says the danger is over now, and that I should be captain of our mess within two weeks.

I have become so afraid of being touched during the night that I dare not sleep. I do not know who is touching me, or tearing my nightdress. There are many things I cannot talk about. During the day I am sleepy and forgetful. How many times I have tried to write to my mother and thrown every sheet away. I am also unable to find the letters I have been writing to Polly.

Beth was discovered up on deck during the night with Sly Joe and someone reported her to Matron. Beth has been confined to steerage for two days. She has barely stopped weeping since. She is so angry, she says she will pour dirty washing water down into the sailor's beds. Indeed, I do not know how she can bear to spend the days downstairs where the air is like steam. During the night we all sleep without blankets in the lightest nightdresses we can find. Even if I were not terrified of being harmed during the night, it would be impossible to sleep with moisture dripping down my back and my head throbbing. Now my bruises have begun to fade and my nightdress has not been torn again.

Lydia has been asking about Richard. She tells me she will carry my secrets with her to the grave. She looks so serious when she says this that I think she must be joking so I laugh. She asks with such understanding that I am coming to trust her. I have begun to tell her what happened. I feel great relief at sharing my own story; for there has never been anyone to confide in. In Shropshire everyone had their own reasons for wanting to know about everyone else's lives. No one was a stranger. But here people only know what I tell them. I can leave out the things I do not like to think about or the things I do not understand. We tell stories to pass the time. We learn to listen well. Lydia believes the purpose of a long voyage is to tell people the stories that could not be told at home.

'Some people are cursed,' she says, 'but tragedy does not have to mean misery.'

ON VERY HOT days, we bathed. I was frightened at first, but watched Richard swim. 'Come on, Sarah,' he said, while William dived. 'There is nothing like water to cool your blood!' Richard captivated me and caused me to forget everything but the present moment. With a hint of guilt, I waded in slowly, my heavy dress slapping my ankles. When the river was up to my waist, I allowed my knees to buckle and gasped as my shoulders fell beneath the water.

'Sarah?' Richard called in alarm. 'Now, pull your arms through the water . . . that's it . . .'

LYDIA LIVED WITH her mother and father. She spent her days nursing her mother; her three older sisters visited occasionally on Sundays. Their mother was ill for some months prior to Lydia's departure.

'I sang to her. It was the only thing that made her smile, Sarah,' she said.

Her father stopped sleeping as his wife's condition worsened. He rarely left her bedside and shared the nursing with his youngest daughter. His skin turned grey.

On entering the sickroom one morning, Lydia found her father's stiff body slumped on the floor. She shook him and slapped his cheeks. She sobbed while her mother whined for coolness.

Her sister Jane arranged their father's funeral while

Lydia cared for their mother. She could not find the words to tell her mother that her father had died.

'I would like to stay here awhile,' Lydia told her sister Jane at the funeral. The vicar spoke words she did not hear. People turned briefly to look at her on their way out the gate as she sat on the ground at the head of the coffin.

As the moon began to glow in the greying sky, she heard a voice.

'Would you like me to come back tomorrow?' a thin man wearing clothes too big for him asked through crooked teeth. Lydia saw that he was holding a shovel.

'Oh,' she stood quickly. 'May I?'

The man laughed. 'No work for a woman!' he said.

'Please. I would like to.'

The man was surprised at the strength in her body. Her round hips balanced her solidly and she shovelled the earth with ease. Finally, she flattened the earth with her hands.

'There,' she panted, wiping her forehead. She knew her face was streaked with dirt but she did not try to wipe herself clean. She sat on the freshly dug grave while tears ran down her cheeks.

Lydia continued to nurse her mother. In the afternoons while her mother slept, she went to the cemetery. She was never there for very long before the man appeared. He allowed her to sit for as long as she liked. Whenever she looked around, she found him pulling limp weeds from the graves. He would rinse his hands in a bucket, wipe them on his trousers and smile. Then he would take one of her hands in his and lead her slowly round the cemetery. He taught Lydia not to be afraid of death. It signalled a change, he said, not an ending. He told her stories of the dead. The people buried in Saint Andrew's, he said, were the most interesting people ever to have lived in England.

She began spending entire afternoons in the cemetery with the man. One night as it grew cold, she turned to leave and he clasped his arms around her body. She felt suddenly warm and comfortable. They spent the whole night draped under the leaves of a willow tree in each other's arms.

When Lydia pushed open the door, sharp fingernails gripped her wrist and dragged her to the kitchen. Jane pushed her through the doorway.

'Where on earth have you been?' she demanded. The two top buttons on Lydia's mourning dress were undone.

'Our mother is dying,' Jane began to sob, 'and you are out . . . doing . . .'

The following morning Jane said that she and her husband were moving into the house to look after Lydia and her mother. 'You are not to leave the house without permission,' Jane told Lydia.

Four months later the man's face turned white as she told him what had happened. He promised to take her away. But when she returned the next day, he had left without her. She could not tell her family or friends why she needed to leave England. Draped in a long shawl, she slipped quietly away by moonlight.

ELIZA HAS BROUGHT the biggest mirror out of all of us. 'It will not break,' she says, 'and even if it does, I have already had seven years of bad luck and that was unconnected with any mirror!' Occasionally someone approaches her to borrow it. We want to see what the salt and the moisture have done to the skin on our faces. Eliza says that we all look younger. If we spent years on the ocean, perhaps our bodies would become youthful enough to live forever—but we would still have to remain clear of disease and disaster. Eliza plucks wiry strands of her own dark hair and sits with the mirror on her lap. In semi-darkness she slips the strand between her teeth. She says there is enough fur growing inside her mouth to make a coat.

I have noticed Eliza preparing strange solutions at the dining table in the evenings. She says that mercury, subnitrate of bismuth and bicarbonate of soda combined with emulsion of almonds will remove the excess colouring from her face. Her skin smells like honey when she comes to say goodnight. When she kisses me her cheeks are white powder.

The jib-boom has snapped at last and we have lost the use of some of the stays. Rope hangs in a limp, indelicate fashion. Like a woman, the vessel is inadequately clad without her stays. She is unable to take full advantage of currents. The captain is becoming concerned about the welfare of the ship. He curses the carpenter behind his back and says that even he could have repaired the jib-boom by now. One of the girls overheard the captain say that the ship is a *gone goose*. I fear it is me who is being punished.

Matron only permits us to speak to each other if we do not make too much noise. We have invented a game where we tell each other stories. It is called, 'Tell Me, Do'. Yesterday I sat still while the others chanted quietly,

Tell me, tell me, Sarah, do,
Where are we going to?'

I smiled. 'Where the waves break,' I said.

It is so long since we saw waves break. The captain says we have occasionally neared land, but if this is true then we have only done so when the unmarried women were below deck. I have not seen foam on waves since the day at Birkenhead. I imagine the New World to be fringed with beautiful rock carvings made by waves with the strength of pounding axes. The rocks are curled into sharp peaks, dark reflections of waves the moment before they crash. The water is a deep blue and the foam, like snow, sprinkles for miles.

I told a story about a large island where women can go barefoot. There are warm caves where we can light fires and sing together. There are no savages to be afraid of.

'And what will you do there?' Charlotte asked. I blushed.

'Tell me, tell me, Beth, do,
Where are we going to?'

'Where the wild men are.'

Beth's forehead creased as she began to tell her story.

Immigrants barely arrive when the wild men board the vessel and take the women away. They are tall and strong, they do not listen to our screams and our kicking barely bruises their skin. They carry us on their backs, wading through the water while our own men run around the deck, taking up and then dropping their weapons, unsure of what to do next.

The wild men carry us and we faint in their arms from fear. They walk for days until we have lost all sense of direction and have moved far beyond the shore where our own men can find us. Then, one by one, we open our eyes and find that we are in a primitive camp. They do not want to hurt us, Beth says. We see their naked wives and children. The women feed small pieces of charred meat into our mouths with rough fingers. They give us water to drink and strange grasses to chew. At first we fear poison, but after some days we become accustomed to their food.

The land is arid. Without the savages we are unable to survive. So we remain. Bored, exhausted. Weeks later, our own men arrive with weapons. But they do not need to use them, for the savages surrender us immediately. They smile and wave as we leave. We return to the town with superior knowledge.

'Beth, what will you do there?'

'I will become a servant to a rich man who pays me good wages and provides me with a large room and ample food. And when I become tired of working for him, I will find another rich man to work for!'

'Oh, Beth.' Eliza shook her head and smiled.

'*Tell me, tell me, Charlotte, do*
Where are we going to?'
'To the place where wild animals are.'

Charlotte giggled as she began. In the New World, she said, women construct armour of gold to protect themselves and the men from dangerous animals. There are tarantulas, with bodies the size of a man's head and legs a foot long. They have fangs and they scream like a child before sinking their teeth into human flesh. Poisonous snakes can be up to a mile long. They need not make use of their venom, but can choke the life from a person in a split second. Their venom does not affect the savages, but white people die instantly. In fact, savages communicate with these dangerous animals in such a way that they are able to train them to collect their food.

So people in the New World wear odd clothes. They have boots of gold that reach up to their thighs. Women rarely wear dresses and cannot even be distinguished from men.

'What will you do there, Charlotte?'

'I will marry my miner and live dazzled by gold!' We all laughed.

'*Tell me, tell me, Liza, do,*
Where are we going to?'
'To the place where we can be alone.'

Eliza barely looked up from her stitching as she told her story. The New World, she said, is a place of great liberation where one need not talk to another person for weeks if one does not wish to.

The land is covered in trees, she said. Twisted, dusty green trees that know the brightness of the light and the harshness of the wind. The local government issues land to almost any person who applies, Eliza said. Even people who used to be prisoners. She will apply for her own land as soon as she arrives.

Charlotte laughed, 'But Eliza, surely they will not give land to a woman?'

'They give land to people who used to be *prisoners*,' she repeated. 'You only need to prove that you will make good use of it.'

Eliza says she will clear the land to build a wooden hut of her own. She will keep some animals and grow vegetables. She will have a spare bedroom so that any of us can visit her whenever we choose.

Some days ago, Matron said there was to be a dance for the unmarried women on board. I was surprised to hear that she was considering allowing some of the sailors to attend. Beneath the poop we grew excited as we imagined dancing with men again. It is so long since I was near any man other than Doctor Carpenter or Mr Greenwood, that I am forgetting how to behave. I can no longer recall whether or not it is proper to meet a man's eye or to smile at him. I have forgotten what it is that one discusses with a man. I must try to remember, for if I should forget myself I shall have to live upon the vessel in shame until we reach the New World.

We fashioned decorations from writing paper. Eliza

allowed us to use a little of her paint when the vessel did not rock. I shredded a sheet of paper into a twisted chain, which I decorated with blue spots and hung across our berth from Charlotte's bed to mine. The longer we spend upon the vessel, the duller we become and the duller the hues of our possessions. These decorations come as a welcome change to our eyes that rarely see colours other than grey and brown. Lydia hung fat red roses from bedposts. The mood below the poop was transformed. We laughed more frequently and moved with lighter steps. But I was anxious to find that, after a month at sea, my ankles, as solid as tree stumps, would be too weak to dance.

Dances became our main topic of conversation. Beth said she preferred waltzing but when Charlotte heard this she was shocked.

'Everyone knows waltzing is improper,' she said, 'for it requires too much intimacy with one's partner. If a woman is not careful, she finds herself leaning heavily on the shoulder of a man. It is too dangerous to be so close to a man that you feel the air currents from his chest caressing your cheek.'

I said nothing when I heard this, for I remembered even Mother and Father waltzing. Beth said she had learned the correct version of the polka with her mother in Paris, and that it was made up of three steps at a pace slightly slower than a gallop. Charlotte said that the French do not know how to dance.

On the evening of the dance, a section of the poop was cleared while two girls from each berth arranged the decorations. Three oil lamps were hung from the masts and the paper decorations were tied around the rigging.

We helped each other dress. My cleanest gown was one with a faint checked pattern in navy blue and green, only slightly creased from the voyage. It was difficult to dress in near darkness with so little standing room. The fabric stuck to my skin in the heat. Lydia was feeling unwell and decided not to attend but stood behind me, pulling the laces of the corset around my waist while I tried to move my arms to the side to avoid hitting Charlotte, who was assisting Beth in front of me.

I sat on Lydia's bed while she twisted my hair and pinned it around my head.

'Turn around,' she muttered through the pin between her teeth. The vessel rocked gently as I put my hands to the dusty boards above the bed and turned to face her.

'You are five years older, Sarah.' She stroked my cheek. 'And you have the golden crown of royalty.'

Since the ocean has been calm, the tiny ocean on the boards has almost dried up. It is strange to walk from one berth to another without feeling a drop of moisture.

We take less and less time in dressing. Matron has difficulty in making us rise in the mornings and we barely have time to button our dresses before breakfast. Although we are careful to dress appropriately, we are lapsing in our attention to physical appearance. As Lydia tightened my corset, it was comforting to feel the proper solidness around my waist once more. It made me believe my body had strength, and encouraged me to think that I would soon return to civilised life. When we spend all our time together, it almost seems pointless to bother dressing and combing our hair, for we are becoming familiar with each other's natural untidiness. I know the shadows under Eliza's eyes as well as I know my own melancholy; the shape of Charlotte's thin hips are as familiar as my own thoughts.

RICHARD AND WILLIAM went to boarding school when I was twelve. During the long months without them, Polly and I were left to attend lessons with Miss Tucker. In the evenings we would make up stories about boarding-school life. Mother often complained about how rarely the boys wrote. We only received letters from them once every few months. It was during those years of being left at home in the schoolroom that I first felt bored with being trapped in Father's house. Everything of interest happened outside.

LAST NIGHT IT was liberating to find myself in the sea air once more. There was a crescent moon and the poop was dimly lit. We were shy in the beginning as we stood around in small clusters peering outwards in an attempt to recognise girls from other berths. Suddenly a long nasal sound of slightly uneven pitch began below the masts. A

Scottish sailor was playing a pipe called the snap. His cheeks blew up like rising pastry and his fingers moved with great independence. He tapped his right foot as he played. The sound was meandering, deeply vibrating and nasal.

'Where are the men?' Beth asked with irritation. The only men to be seen were the musician and Doctor Carpenter, who stood near Matron thumping his belly with the forefinger of his right hand.

I saw that a group of Irish girls had taken off their boots and stockings and were hopping around in a circle holding hands. Matron was talking to Doctor Carpenter and did not notice.

'It's the Schottische!' someone shouted, and someone else took my left hand while I clasped Eliza's with my right.

The monkey poop was transformed in the moonlight and I felt as though I danced in an immense ballroom with chandeliers. My body and mind grew so light that I thought I might float to the stars.

As the tempo of the music changed, Beth decided to teach us the polka. She took my left hand with her right and we began to move towards each other. We faced each other briefly and then turned; Beth jumped and gave a small kick. We then continued to move together in a circle in front of Charlotte and Eliza.

We had fallen into step with each other. Then I realised that a group of Scottish girls were standing to the side glaring at us.

'That's nort the polka!' one of them said. 'This is how ya do it.'

We took little notice as they formed their own circle next to ours. By now there were more of us and we skipped as we moved in towards the centre.

'D'ya hearr?' another girl said, her voice rising in anger. 'I'll punch yer head in!' We were no longer exactly in time. My ankles were beginning to feel light once more as I swung around the poop with the other girls. All of a sudden, someone wrenched our hands apart and I slipped on the deck. Limbs flew in all directions.

Someone pulled me up by the hands before pushing me firmly towards the hatchway stairs.

'Time for bed, off you go . . .' Doctor Carpenter's voice said.

There was groaning and sniffling. We formed an untidy queue as we stumbled, disappointed, back down into the darkness.

'I CAN TELL the future from the clouds,' Richard said one day. I was fourteen. It was summer and we lay on our backs on the hill leading down to the river. The sunshine was too bright for me to open my eyes. I saw orange inside my eyelids. I felt as though someone was warming my skin, blowing and stroking.

'How?' I asked.

'By interpreting the pictures,' he said.

'Why should a cloud speak to you alone?'

'That cloud over there is yours, Sarah.'

'Why?'

'No one else has claimed it.'

'Richard!' I reached out my hand and found his left arm.

For a few seconds he said nothing.

'What does it say?' The light filtered through my eyelashes made my eyes water.

'It is moving quickly across the sky.'

'What does that mean?'

'A voyage.'

I laughed. 'Where am I going? I'll be lucky to get the railway to London!'

'You will travel, Sarah.' Richard's voice was so serious that I sat up. He waited for me to speak. I blinked and saw crimson spots.

'Where will I go?' I whispered.

He looked at the grass between us. He stared at it as though he expected it to speak. He lifted his left hand to his mouth and shook his head.

⁓

EVEN UNDER THE corset I have the stature of a tree stump. I have the limbs of a boy who spends his days in the fields. Before I left Shropshire, my fingers had the thickness of peasants' hands but the strength to draw music from the tiniest of pianofortes. Mother bought me gloves for the Spring Ball last year with white fingers far longer than mine. She had forgotten that I do not yet have her hands.

Polly played the pianoforte for the first part of the evening. I spoke to Mr Peterson. During an interval, Mother beckoned me to her.

'Sarah, you must dance. We did not arrange this ball for you to spend the entire evening *conversing*.'

'I will play now, Mother. Polly may dance.'

'No. You must be sociable.'

I held my lips in a tight thin line and noticed Mr Downing watching from his seat near Polly. He tried to curve his lips into a smile and stood to walk towards me. Mother smiled at him.

'Mr Downing,' Mother said. 'So kind of you to dance with my daughter.'

He gripped the fabric of my gloves without realising I did not fill them. His hand around my waist made me frightened to take in air.

'You must come to my estate.' He blew cheese-breath into my face. 'We will go punting, Sarah. Punting. Marvellous occupation. Have you seen a man punt before?'

'No,' I muttered.

'That settles it then. A weekend in spring. Lovely.'

My neck was beginning to ache and the room spun.

'Excuse me, I do not feel well . . . must sit down.'

I opened my eyes to find myself lying on my back with Mother, Polly, and Mr Downing peering down at me. The music had stopped and people were whispering anxiously.

'She has come to. Stand, Sarah.' Mother pulled me to my feet. 'Polly, continue your playing. People should dance . . .'

Mother led me from the drawing room. 'What is wrong with you, Sarah?' Mother pleaded. 'Why must you always make a scene and draw attention to yourself?'

By the end of the evening, the silk gloves had sucked the life from my palms. I waved fabric rather than flesh to all our guests as they made their way to their carriages.

~~~

UNTIL I LEARNED about Grandmother Fryer's hair, I thought I understood the line of women in my family. One evening Mother began to tell me more about the grandparents. It was time I understood the pattern, she said.

It seemed that my mother and my grandmother were extraordinary in different, unspeakable ways. But there was an important link between them. It was a question of disguise. Grandmother Fryer had passed on to my mother the precious gift of knowing how to pretend.

I had to learn how to read the signs. So, a week after my fifteenth birthday Mother spoke with me alone. It was a Friday evening and we made our way to her room. I felt that I was being divulged a secret that was so large I could only absorb small droplets at a time. As Mother led me by the hand from the dining room, Polly pulled her lips into a tight thin line and stared. Father peered harder than ever at the pages of his grandfather's bible. I often thought Father must have been searching for a secret of his own in Great-Grandfather's bible, for he would read it several times a week even though he knew the passages by heart.

On our way to Mother's room we passed Florrie dusting the teacup collection in the hall and Mother smiled. 'We are not to be disturbed, Florrie,' she said.

'Come, sit down,' Mother told me on that first Friday evening, pointing to the window seat where I had always longed to sit as a child. Now that I was being invited into a place previously prohibited, I did not feel at ease. While I made my way slowly towards the curtains, I remembered a younger, more frightened Florrie running after me as I giggled. 'No, Miss,' she had whispered. 'You mustn't go there . . .' As she had lifted me to her right hip I had begun to sob. Everything that was of interest, it seemed, was forbidden.

'Sarah, I hope you have not begun to love,' Mother said. 'You are far too young. You must marry first. Love will come later.' I did not dare to open my mouth for fear words would drip before I could stop them. Mother said that if I felt that I was beginning to love, I needed to marry quickly.

'Are you, Sarah?'

I looked at my hands. 'I do not know, Mother.' I felt blood rising to my cheeks.

'And Mr Downing? I hope he does not know this.'

'No, Mother.'

I thought of the leathery skin on his face and the bristles that grew like weeds on his chin. I shuddered and remembered the church picnic when Richard had been absent. Mr Downing's arms had been like rope around my waist.

'Sarah, you must not break the pattern,' she said. 'You will marry Mr Downing.'

'Mother!'

'He will provide for you, Sarah. That is what marriage is for. After the wedding, you will have time to find a man to love silently. But not until then. Sarah, you cannot love now. It is far too dangerous.'

WE WASHED OUR clothes on the deck a few days ago. Salt water is as good as starch but it shrivels the skin. We move so slowly, wringing in unison, watching grime brown the water in the washing pans. There is nowhere else to hang our clothes but from the masts. We must ask the sailors to do so, and we stare at the deck as they tie our drawers with twine to the ropes. There is little wind. Matron slumps on the chicken coop in a most unladylike fashion, fanning herself with her sun hat as the sailors smile and chant, 'Ya-ho-hup-la-haul-there-ha-ho-now-ho-hup-la-Betsy-ha-ho'. Their voices come as relief through the silence. We laugh when our drawers hang limply as death. When the breeze comes along we will be propelled by our underclothes. Our drawers will fill and move like ghosts.

Matron said it would not do for us to slump around on deck in the heat like so many sacks of flour. On the poop we are in full view of the other passengers, so we must be seen to be maintaining a routine. 'You have no prospects at all if you do not find a husband,' she says. Matron believes that men will be allured by marching feet. 'Women who walk draw men to their heels like flies to rotting meat.'

She demands that we march around the deck twenty times each morning like a school parade. She does not walk with us, but instead stands outside the captain's cabin and shouts orders each time we walk by.

'Charlotte, walk more elegantly! No man will ever wish to be seen with such a lizard! Elizabeth, straighten your back!'

The sailors laugh and call us the Ragged Army. Only those feeling ill are permitted to sit quietly without exerting themselves; now it is but ten who march. When the marching is over, we sit dripping under our bonnets. Anyone who has misbehaved must fan Matron with the pages of a book.

Charlotte has discovered something of particular note to me—that Sally and Susan from the berth next to ours have a brother in the men's accommodation. He has been sick with typhus for a week and the girls are not permitted to visit him. They long to be able to care for him, to make arrowroot over a lamp and wash his stained bedclothes. They know it is what their mother would expect them to do for him. This is what their own mother did for their father during the several months that he was bedridden before he died. Sally weeps and says that she wants to be permitted to tell him stories. She believes that if she makes him think of events other than his illness, he will gain the strength to cure himself.

WHEN MOTHER FIRST began to show me the remembrances of the grandparents, it was after Captain Fryer's vessel had been shipwrecked on the Cornwall coast. In memory of Captain Fryer, Grandmother Fryer had had a mourning box carved from the ship's oak. Mother snapped the box open and looked into my eyes silently. Her gaze returned to the box.

'Here.' She pulled out a brown object that moved of its own accord like an eel. I tried to smile but was having trouble breathing. The object was a hollow coil constructed from fine brown netting and curved into a spiral that looked as though it would strangle the life from a woman's body. I could feel a tremor beginning in my chest and working its way down my spine.

'Grandmother's hair,' she said.

It was around that time that I began to have vivid dreams. In one of them, a man whose face I did not know was knotting my hair into a coil while my scalp bled. In another, Grandmother screamed at me with red eyes. 'Are you so ungrateful for my gifts that you will not remain part of this family?' she demanded while I sobbed in a puddle of tears. In the final dream, *my* hair came to life and began to weave into netting of its own accord. With each layer of knots, the coil became more animated until it wove tightly around my neck. When I woke I was tied in torn sheets knotted together. In the morning when Florrie came to help me dress I lay on the naked bed shivering. 'Please don't tell Mother,' I asked her. She nodded quickly.

A few days later, Mother took me to her room again. I needed to see the patterns of women, she repeated. Only this way would I understand how I needed to behave. I feared that she would ask me about love again, or would wish to talk about Mr Downing. I dreaded having to tell her of my own pattern; how it had begun when I was ten and was now too strong to be broken.

I sat with my shoulders back on the window seat, watching Mother.

'Here,' she muttered breathlessly, 'Grandfather's mourning box.' It was shaped like a coffin, carved with anchors and sails. It could have held three of Great-Grandfather's bibles stacked lying down. I shuddered, not wanting to see any more of what was inside. I longed to listen to Father reading from the bible, or to play hide and seek with Polly in the drawing room.

I DISCOVERED TWO of the letters I have written to Polly hidden under Annie's pillow. Even though there has been no chance to send them, I was angry. I left them there and waited until she was in bed.

'What do you mean by stealing my letters?' I wrenched the pillow from under her head. But the letters had gone.

'What would I want your letters for?'

'You tell me, you beast!' I began to punch her and she squealed.

'Stop! It wasn't me!'

'It was you who tore my nightdress and bit me during the night, wasn't it?' I pulled a tuft of hair from her head and scratched her arm with a fingernail. Dark liquid began to flow from her nose where I had hit her. I could smell smoke and the berth was suddenly light.

'Sarah!' Someone pulled my arms behind my back and held them firmly while I tried to pull free.

'Matron,' Annie began to sob. 'Matron, Sarah has been going up on deck during the night. I think she has been seeing one of the sailors. I wake up and she is never here . . .'

Matron's eyes were hard as porcelain as she glared at me. Suddenly I felt that she knew everything I had done. She was going to make sure I was punished. I shuddered and stared helplessly at her.

'Is this true, Sarah?' she asked.

'No, Annie took—'

'The longer it is that you lie to me, the longer you will remain below deck.'

'It was Annie who—'

'You must both learn to be polite to each other and you, Sarah, must come to me when you are ready to tell the truth. Until then, you are not permitted on deck with the others.'

I deliberately thrashed about during the night, hoping to cover Annie in bruises. The next day I felt like a convict. I lay for hours in a sweat thinking I would flood the vessel. Everything that had been so neatly contained within me was going to multiply, spill and run. My thoughts were dangerous because I could no longer control them. They were dark and violent. The only sounds were faint footsteps and voices on the poop. The noise was far away. There was room in the berths for my mind and thoughts to expand. I imagined that my body was growing so that it took up all the room below the deck. I slept very deeply. Upon waking I thought I was in the darkness beneath the sea. Then I realised it was so hot that I was losing my mind.

On the second afternoon, Charlotte came below deck and knelt next to my bed. 'You can come out, Sarah,' she whispered. 'Matron says you can come out as long as you apologise for your behaviour. Please come, Sarah. You will die down here. It still smells so awful. And the heat, Sarah.'

Lying on my bed, I felt that I was on an abandoned ship. I wondered whether anyone would let me know if we were sinking. Even without the other unmarried women, the berths were cluttered with crumpled bedding and dirty clothes. But at least the air beneath the poop was my own.

As I pulled myself into a sitting position the berths swirled around my head. I had to sit still for several minutes before summoning the faith that my limbs would allow me to stand. Pacing the berths three times, I passed Eliza's neatly made bed, Lydia's bed draped in one of her shawls, and Charlotte's nightdress with the lace collar poking out from her canvas bag. I discovered the pig snuffling under the dining table, her bell ringing softly, and found a shrivelled carrot to feed her. There was a small book on Beth's bed. I walked past it twice. The third time, I stopped, peered up and down the passage, and picked up the book. It no longer mattered how many rules I broke. Matron would make sure I was punished.

My fingers shook so violently that I was worried I would tear the pages. The handwriting reflected the motion of the ship. The opening pages described Beth's illness on boarding the vessel. I flipped to the middle of the book. As I began to make out the words, I was astonished to discover what Beth had written about the Albatross Man. She described how she had gone to visit him in the ship hospital. Like the men, she had dropped him a fish and then he had fallen at her feet in appreciation. He cooed to her, she had written, until the softness of his voice had almost sent her to sleep. When she lay on his bed and he stood, flapping his wings beside her, he began to tell stories of soaring through the heavens. Beth had written that the Albatross Man had taken her to paradise.

When I read this, my heart began to pound so loudly that I feared it would bring the others running. I pressed the pages of the book closed, and laid it on the corner of Beth's bed in the exact position I had found it. Holding my arms firmly around my chest, I moved slowly back towards my bed. My breathing was uneven. I knew that if I did not drink soon, I would faint.

I tried to comb the stickiness from my hair. Strands broke and shredded as I tugged at them. I left it tangled and pulled it back tightly behind my head. I knew my temples would soon ache from the strain of the knot. In the evening when Matron herded the other girls down into steerage once more, I approached her before Annie reappeared. I could not bear to look into her eyes as I apologised for something I had not done. Matron touched my left arm so that I jumped in surprise.

'You must be careful, Sarah,' she said softly. 'Much harm can come to a girl on this voyage.'

I have noticed that Annie is always muttering hurriedly to herself. She does this with particular attention after she has gone to bed. One night I lay on my stomach with my right ear towards her so that I could make out what she was saying.

'Four thousand and thirty-five . . . four thousand and thirty-six . . . four thousand and thirty-seven . . .'

I sighed. 'Annie, what are you doing?'

'Counting.'

'Why?'

'I am passing the time. I am training my body to tell the time so that I will not be reliant on being told any longer. Do you know that if you count to three thousand six hundred then an hour will pass?'

After that conversation with Annie, I found that my own mind became frequently filled with numbers. I wondered if I could count to eighty-six thousand four hundred to make a day pass. Every evening before going to sleep I pulled out pieces of paper and made more calculations of seconds. There would be over twenty-four million seconds in a month. If we were aboard the ship for three months, I would have to count to over seventy-two and a half million.

It fascinated me that there existed enough numbers to carry us to the New World without having to repeat the same number twice. That all I had to do was concentrate and learn how to say the big numbers quickly so that their utterance did not take up more than a second, and I could count us to land. The problem was that while Annie could count up to thousands in a day, I found that I could never get up to more than seven hundred or so before someone would ask me a question or something would happen on board to distract me from counting. I frequently had to start again because I had forgotten what number I was up to. After a couple of days, I gave up trying to count the seconds of our voyage. But every night when I lay in my bed, Annie's numbers muttered their way into my mind.

Our Irish neighbours are very noisy now. The cadences of their voices are so similar that I cannot tell whether or not I am hearing the same people. A wafer of wood separates my berth from theirs. I have never seen them. But sometimes I imagine the barrier is glass. The wife screeches at her husband and once they had a falling out where he gave her a thrashing. I could hear her screaming while fists thumped flesh. Then there was silence until the man began to pant and whisper, 'Mary. Speak to me, Mary.'

It was some time later that I heard dripping water and strained whispering. Then Doctor Carpenter's voice pushed through the wall,

'If you do this again, I'll bind you to the mast and flog you.'

One morning I was tying Lydia's hair into a bun when something tickled my fingers. I did not wish to alarm her but said I wanted to put some flowers in her hair. On the monkey poop I fashioned roses from paper and as I bent to pin them in her hair, I saw something move.

'Lydia,' I whispered so the others would not hear. 'I think you have lice.'

Lydia jumped from the seat, almost dropping her shawl while her stitching fell to the deck, her cheeks turning crimson.

'Has something bitten you, Lydia?' Emily from the mess next to ours joked. Suddenly I noticed that my head was also beginning to itch.

We have all been infested with vermin from one of those Irish families in the neighbouring mess. There is now little shame as we sit on deck, a line of girls all pulling small metal combs painfully through the hair of the girl in front of us. Our hair is becoming rough as twine and stiff from salt. It sticks together in tangled curls or in long thin tails. We fear we will never again have smooth shiny locks. We snatch long strands of fair hair, wiry strands of black, and finger-length strands of brown to short, sharp cries. We squeeze the small eggs with disgust between our fingers.

Matron has said that if we are unable to rid each other of lice within two days, we shall all have to receive treatment. I think the creatures have been sent to test me. Our hair will be soaked in kerosene for twenty-four hours and fresh oil is to be added to the solution three times. We shall then have to bind our hair in rags overnight before washing the chemicals from our heads. On top of the foul-smelling water rising like smoke from the bowels of the ship, I could not bear the smell of kerosene. I fear that soaking in the chemical would cause me to catch on fire when passing an oil lamp, and that I would end my days flaring dramatically in the sky.

Doctor has ordered the family to be removed from steerage. As they were being led away, the woman flung the contents of a bucket into our quarters. We were all sprinkled in mud. She retched and spat at Annie.

They have been housed in a cabin that was previously disused on account of it having a slight opening in the porthole, allowing a certain amount of water in. I have heard that all members of that benighted family have had their hair cropped, they were scrubbed on the deck with salt water under the supervision of Doctor Carpenter himself. Their bedding was thrown overboard.

It is of some relief that this could never happen to us. English girls would never be treated in the same manner as a poor Irish family.

A WEEK AFTER Mother first began to show me the remembrances of Grandmother, she tried to catch my eye at dinner. I stared at my potatoes and wondered what Mabel would bring for sweets.

'Come, Sarah,' Mother said when we had finished eating.

I sat on the window seat and clasped my hands together in my lap to hide the trembling, while Mother opened the trunk.

'I want you to touch the coil and think of Grandmother,' she said. 'You should become familiar with these objects before they are yours. See how delicate the work is. The neatness of the pattern. Feel the lightness of the fabric . . . nothing more smooth than human hair.'

The legacy of Grandmother Fryer was netting. It could be used to catch small fish. And I imagined Grandmother lying embalmed in her coffin with the engraving and the shiny brass handles. I saw her maids unwinding the huge plait that had remained a faint shade of copper and had been wound around her head since she was a child. It rippled like murky water. I could see their fingers deftly unplaiting the rope of hair while Grandmother lay still and silent with a faint grin on her face. Would they have been nervous, making such a final gesture as to remove the hair from the body? Would they have feared the sight of Grandmother with untidily cropped waves? Perhaps Grandmother's spirit lay in her hair, and to cut it was to complete her earthly death. To remain tied around future generations of women had been my grandmother's dying wish.

'The most precious remembrance of Grandmother.' She had coiled the eel of hair back inside the box and held a tiny glistening object in her hand. 'A mourning brooch,' she said.

There was nothing horrible in that first glance. A small oval-shaped ring of gold, framed in tiny pearls. 'The tears of the ocean,' Mother said. But as I peered more closely, I could see that something underneath the glass cover was moving. Mother dropped it in my hand and it felt warm and pulsing with life. Underneath the glass was a tiny mat of tightly woven hair that throbbed in the light. The brooch was hung from a golden chain attached to a pin. As I held the golden shell, I knew that the hair inside was still growing.

I longed to give what was left of Grandmother Fryer back to Mother.

'When we make decisions, Sarah,' Mother began, 'we must think of the good of the entire family. Take this brooch and the hair.'

I hid them in an old pair of gloves in the top of my wardrobe. During the night, Grandmother's hair whistled in the wind. The chain rattled and the pin grew until it was long and sharp enough to pierce my body.

~

ELIZA IS UNWELL. She has been ill a number of days now, but there is not room for her in the ship hospital. Doctor Carpenter visits her every few days, and says we must try to keep her fever down. It is difficult to do so when everywhere is hot. I have been bathing her forehead with a flannel soaked in sea water; her skin is becoming dry and rough. She is grateful for lime juice; I give her mine as well, in the rough tin cup. Occasionally I also make arrowroot for her over the lamp at the dining table. It is days since she was able to eat. I fear for her and wish there was something I could do to make her strong again.

She is a gentle invalid and does not ever weep or complain. Sometimes she touches my hand and says, 'Father, I will bring in the horses.' One of the ship's cats has found its way onto her bed, and no matter how many times I remove him, he always returns to her. He stretches himself against her back and, while I fear he will make the heat unbearable for her, she seems comforted by his presence.

I am not sure that Eliza hears me, but I feel it is important to talk to her. I tell her stories to remind her of things that have happened. I begin by recalling the singing competition that was held last week. That was the first time we were allowed on deck in the evening with all the other passengers. The sky burned a brilliant orange and the sun sank a glowing gold into the ocean. I barely heard the first few singers; my heart was clanging in my ears as I searched everywhere for Richard. I thought I saw him standing behind a sailor, but then Lydia elbowed me because Eliza was singing and her magical voice floated over our heads and into the sea. When she sang 'Do they miss me at home', even some of the men reached for their handkerchiefs. I feel sure that Eliza would have won the competition that evening if it wasn't for Rebecca Brown having such an angelic face and dressing in a silk gown to perform 'Hard times come ye again no more'. We thought the prize was to be a delicate writing desk built by the carpenter and were somewhat disappointed to discover that this was the prize for the best male singer. Indeed, Eliza said that she was glad not to be awarded the albatross-skin purse that was given to Rebecca.

If I am very good, if I give Eliza all I have, perhaps God will forgive me for all I have done.

~

MOTHER NEVER MENTIONED her youth without talking about the two brothers. When she met Father at a ball, Uncle Frederick was already married. But his wife was weak, Mother said. Aunt Isabel had little energy for her husband. In his loneliness, Uncle Frederick frequently accompanied Father on his visits to Mother. Uncle Frederick was a lawyer by then, and he spent his days shuffling pages and stories. Mother married Father because she believed that he shared her desire for dryness.

My mother said Aunt Isabel died when Richard was born and Uncle Frederick was so grieved that no one has dared mention her since. On the few occasions that I visited the cottage in Shropshire, it had an air of emptiness about it. There were no objects to indicate that a woman had ever lived there at all. It was as though someone had meticulously collected all of Aunt Isabel's belongings and burned them to ash. The interior was bereft of a gentle touch. The house was so barren that I could not imagine any person to have been born there.

I long to see Richard and to ask him again about my mother's stories. I am sure that he will know how many of them are true. Sometimes I think that he is the only person I will ever be able to trust.

~

WE HAVE HEARD that the brother of the two girls in the neighbouring berth has died of typhus. Matron did not permit them to visit him at all. They were allowed to see him only covered in a canvas sack before he was dropped into the ocean. Sally says she is not sure that it was in fact her own brother who was committed to the deep.

'I only know of his illness through hearsay,' she said. 'I remember him as strong and travelling with us to London.'

Sally says she will not write to her mother and tell her of the death when she herself is not sure that it is true. Susan, however, has been weeping ever since she first heard the news. She says their mother must know immediately and has already begun to compose the letter.

Matron has allowed the remaining birds to be kept on deck. I am suspicious of this unexpected kindness. Though I fear the death of Poseidon was a bad omen. Perhaps we would now have more control over our own direction if we chanted softly and prayed into the fires below the sea for deliverance from evil. I flick droplets of salt water from my fingers to cool the birds. Artemis drops to the floor of the cage and begins dusting herself slowly with her sharp beak. Lares and Penates stare blindly into the moist air. Even if we opened the cage to set them free, I fear the birds would be too weak to fly and would drown in the ocean.

Since I read her diary, I can no longer look Beth in the eye. When she speaks to me, I know that I blush. She looks at me as though she longs to ask me a question, but thinks better of it. Beth says that Mr Greenwood was caught in Mrs Everston's cabin. I find it difficult to believe such a tale, particularly when I have learned of her own secrets. Yet Mr Greenwood does not come to us any longer. Our new constable is called Mr Hollyworth. He is small and quiet, removing and returning our food with great haste.

It is only a few days since we crossed the line. The sun at midday was stronger than I have seen it before and directly over our heads! I remembered the map of the world hanging in the schoolroom at home, and how Miss Tucker would make me close my eyes to recite the continents and their position. It was after several years of geography that I came to the realisation that latitudes and longitudes were one of man's inventions in order to attempt comprehension. I was disappointed the day I learned that the equator did not really exist. Still, I imagined a line like a rainbow stretched across the sky. As we hovered underneath what must have been the exact point, I searched the horizon for a line that had not been there before. I must write and tell Miss Tucker how far I have come.

As we burned pink under the sun I noticed that everything glowed hot and that there was no shade, even under our bonnets. I wondered where all my shadows had gone. There may be a land made up of nothing but shadows; it is when they creep across to see what our world is like, that we find them. Perhaps I left my shadow with Polly. Or maybe it is ailing with Eliza under the bedclothes.

A few single men caught some of the others and told them it was good luck to be shaved during the crossing. The men sheared the others like fat sheep. We celebrated crossing the line. Some of the men wandered up and down the decks dressed to represent old and new England. Old England was grey and thin with hunger, crying for warmth. New England was a fat man of the bush, his arms spilling bread and cheese, his pockets bulging with gold. We were not permitted to see much of the ceremony. From underneath my blankets I heard raucous singing.

'Sirens in every port we meet,
More fell than rocks or waves;
But such as grace the British fleet,
Are lovers and not slaves.
No foes our courage shall subdue,
Altho' we've left our hearts with you . . .'

AFTER MOTHER SHOWED me Grandmother Fryer's brooch, I dreamed that it anchored me to Mr Downing. That the anchor grew heavy and my skin began to tear. That the chains were wrapped around my body so that I could barely breathe and could not utter words of drowning. That Mr Downing was proud of a new gold habit I wore, and put me in a glass box to show visitors.

Three nights before I left, I could bear it no longer. When I knew that even Florrie had gone to bed, I lit a candle and pulled on my cloak and boots. I stood on a chair and felt for the gloves in the top of my wardrobe. Jumping over the floorboards that creaked, I ran to the kitchen and rattled the iron key in the lock until it opened.

I entered the garden at the moment when the dew began to fall. I breathed dewdrops in through my nose and ran towards the River Severn, trusting my feet to follow the path to church. I almost stepped into the water before I realised I had arrived. The brooch had grown weighty in my hand. I wanted to be free. The first time I tried to toss it into the water, the chain caught in the fabric of my cloak. I heard screaming as I tossed Grandmother Fryer's mourning brooch into the Severn.

The coil had become tied around my wrist and my hands tingled. With the fingers of my right hand I unwound the object from my wrist. *It is twine*, I told myself. *It has never known life*. When I held the end of the coil, the object danced in my fingers. By the moonlight I could see it quiver while I felt a slight tug. I heard faint singing.

Suddenly, the coil gave a great lurch and I slipped on the riverbank. There was a huge splash as my boots hit the water, pulling me after them. As I tumbled into the river, I wondered what Mother would say when she heard that I had drowned trying to be rid of Grandmother Fryer's hair.

I pulled my arms through the water, gasping for air. I could feel thousands of creatures awoken in the darkness in surprise, stroking my limbs and my face. I knew that if I drowned they would feast for months on my flesh. As I began to rise towards the surface, I opened my mouth to breathe. That was when I swallowed the fish. It was quite a small fish, and it slithered down my throat as though it longed to discover what was there.

As I made my way, sniffling, towards the house, I knew that the fish had made a home in my belly. I felt it hitting the insides of my skin. I realised I was water. That when I had been floating in the Severn, it was only a thin layer of my skin that separated the liquid inside me from the liquid outside. I pulled my hair in front of my face and wrung out the water. It was still moving with river life. As I let the hair drop behind my back, I felt something scratch my neck. Grandmother Fryer's hair was stuck to my skin.

Once in my room, I put more kindling on the fire and laid out my clothes to dry. I climbed under the bedclothes. It was then that I knew I preferred salt.

AS ONE OCEAN flows through me, another begins to flow around me. Shells of small creatures have formed tiny grains of sand, sometimes black, on my scalp. I can collect them under my fingernails. The more I try to collect, the more sand forms. When I lie under my sheets during the night and the moist hair flows around my head, I feel that my mind is becoming the ocean floor.

The Doldrum Calms
August 13, 1854

4. Mrs Louisa Garnett
c/- Frederick Garnett, Esq.
'Farraways'
Dorrington
Shropshire

My dear Mother,
      I am frightened . . .

*T*HERE IS NO line between the pale blue of the sky and the sea. They melt into each other and I am floating on air. I breathe the ocean.

The sun draws the energy from our limbs and we are smothered in silence; I cannot even hear lapping water and am unable to ascertain the depth of the ocean because the sea is too still for me to detect a pitch. I hope this does not mean that we are running aground. Perhaps we have been sucked into a deep hole never to emerge. Our souls have continued to live elsewhere while we live with the emptiness of shadows. I fear I am feverish or dead.

For the first few hours of daylight, the heat of the night still drips from my itchy nose. Even the fish in my belly is growing sluggish and no longer wishes to eat. It is sleeping inside me and occasionally when I roll over during the night, it knocks against my sides. It is too lethargic to do me any harm.

Mrs Peacock's infant died of *frog in the mouth*. It is said that she neglected to cover its head with a flannel to protect its ears and eyes from currents of air. For some time the body was still swaddled though the skin was turning grey and stiff. Still, for the few moments whenever Mrs Peacock slept, she held the corpse in her arms. After two days, Doctor Carpenter was sent by the captain to remove the child. He waited until she slept and then tried to peel her fingers away from the body. She woke screaming, her eyes wild. She slashed her fingernails through the air like a cat. Doctor Carpenter leapt backwards to prevent being clawed. She howled for an hour. No one could subdue her; he could not get close enough to give her a dose of laudanum. Her husband grew more and more alarmed. He feared they would lock Mrs Peacock away in a straitwaistcoat until she found herself again. He was worried about what would happen to the other children.

Eventually, she fell silent and stopped thrashing about. She allowed Doctor Carpenter to sit near her. The child needed to be given a Christian burial, he said. She could not deny him that. He held out his arms, and she handed him the body.

She has not been herself since. I have heard that she can no longer keep still, and that even during the night she paces the decks.

ON THE RIVERBANK, Richard used the knife his father had given him to whittle wood. William stared sullenly from under his curls.

'You try,' Richard said, offering my brother the much-prized knife. William's early attempts at carving were weak. Those first ships were barely recognisable from wedges of wood; their sails were constructed from limp oak leaves still attached to their stems.

We spent a whole summer by the Severn and created a fleet of ships, which we hid in the evening behind rocks. Each boat was carved with its own name. While the boys perfected the vessels, I made tiny people out of twigs tied with dried grass. We raced the boats. At first the winning boat seemed to be determined by the strength of the current in that part of the river. Slowly we learned that the shape of the vessel decided its speed. The more pointed and slender the boat, the faster it travelled. However, if the vessel was too thin, it stood great risk of overturning and losing its passengers overboard.

A FEW NIGHTS ago, everyone awoke to Matron's rampaging. She waddled up and down the berths unsteadily, clutching a bottle. In the lamplight I could see that her eyes were clear and she seemed to be in a trance. At first she muttered bitterly.

'Thou broughtest us into the snare: and laidst trouble upon our loins . . . we went through fire and water, and thou broughtest us out into a wealthy place . . .'

Suddenly, her eyes began to scour the berths. 'Clean up this mess!' she shouted as she pushed our books and tins off the dining table. There was a loud thump and harsh ringing as the pig awoke in fright at the noise and hit her head. The animal stood for a few seconds in a daze. Then she pushed past Matron and made her way to the married people's accommodation. I squeezed my eyes closed.

'*I will offer unto thee fat burnt-sacrifices, with the incense of rams: I will offer bullocks and goats.*' I felt the boards tremble as she collapsed on the floor. Through half-open eyes I saw her clutch her stomach and begin to sob. 'Oh, Jonathan . . .' she wailed. After a few moments, Doctor Carpenter arrived and led her quietly away.

I have heard that Matron used to be a wife. Many years ago she was light and full of laughter. She wished to emigrate to the New World with her husband and her three children. At the time of their voyage, Matron's two sons were ten and twelve years old. Her infant was six months. During the voyage, Matron's husband became ill with *water on the brain*. It is said that he ceased to be himself and began to speak as though he were the surgeon who would visit him every afternoon straight after lunch and gently shake his head. Matron's husband walked to his death on the day that he believed they had reached land. He stepped off the vessel and struck his head on the ship as he fell beneath the waves.

Although sailors dived after him, Matron's husband was never found. Her smiles and her laughter drowned with him. Matron believed that he was never far beneath the surface of the water. She paced the decks during the night. Sometimes she would get down on her hands and knees and squint into the sea. She would claim to see his face, his eyeglass or his moustache floating towards her. The doctor began to fear for her health.

While Matron searched for her husband, she left her two sons in the cabin. They were not to make any noise, she instructed. If they misbehaved, she would throw them overboard and they could join their father under the ocean. The two boys did not wish to stay in the cabin with the crying child. They wanted to climb the rigging with the sailors. They begged the captain to show them how to steer the vessel.

One afternoon while Matron was pacing the decks in search of her husband, her sons sat in the cabin with the baby. The infant would not stop screaming. The boys yelled at her to be quiet. They smacked her tiny hands. Her face was raw red and wrinkled. Her cries drowned every other thought out of their heads. The sound grew in the confined space. The boys held their hands over their ears and screwed their eyes shut.

'Mary's misbehaving,' the smaller boy shouted when he had opened his eyes.

'She must be punished,' the older one agreed. 'Lift her up.'

'No, you take her. You're the oldest.'

He lifted his sister for the last time. 'Please be quiet, Mary,' he told her. Her tiny body buzzed with noise. 'Come on,' he told his younger brother.

No one saw the two boys arrive on the poop with the baby, who howled even louder in the cool air. The captain would say later that things always went wrong when he left his vessel in the hands of a sailor. The children scurried towards the bow. Most of the passengers were at the stern of the ship watching for whales.

'It's your turn now.' The older brother handed the screaming child to the other. The small boy flung the swaddled baby into the sea. Her cries were soon muffled by the water.

Matron never forgave her sons. She locked them in the cabin for the remainder of the voyage, letting them out twice a day to use the water closet, and feeding them left-over food from her own plate. Matron left her two sons in the New World and returned to the sea so that she could search constantly for her dead husband and baby.

⁓

ONE OF THE most memorable events of those last few years in Shropshire while the boys were away at school, was the opening of the Shrewsbury and Hereford Railway to Ludlow. Father had been working for some months in assisting the Directors of the Railway, and the arrival of the first train was awaited with great anticipation by all. William and Richard came home from boarding school by carriage for the occasion, and were to return on one of the first trains. Polly and I travelled to Church Stretton with the boys while Mother and Father travelled separately so that they could attend the festival dinner afterwards. Our coach pulled into the town while the bells of the old church tolled to accompany the brass band. We arrived early enough to gain excellent positions on the railway bridge from where to observe the festivities.

After eleven, we noticed that people on the railway platform were beginning to point and that a growing black spot had appeared on the horizon. Before long we could hear the regular chugging of steam growing louder. I cannot put into words my excitement at seeing the carriage that could take me so far away from Shropshire. It looked as though it had the strength to chug all the way to another land. It was a vehicle I could use without having to ask Father if I could take one of the horses. The train could begin an adventure.

We waved handkerchiefs at the carriage as it departed. Many of the Shropshire women were crying.

———

BETH HEARD THAT there was a copy of Mr Wentworth's *Description of the Colony of New South Wales* in the ship library. Doctor Carpenter promised he would borrow it for her and Beth asked him about it every time she saw him. Doctor Carpenter grew very impatient. He said that many people wished to read the book and that it was never anywhere to be found.

One morning, however, Doctor Carpenter arrived and handed Beth the volume. She told me afterwards that she was so happy to see it that she had almost kissed him, but had come to her senses just in time. Doctor Carpenter said that Beth would have to read quickly. He would be collecting it from her the following morning.

'There are many passengers on board who have not even so much as *seen* this volume yet,' he said.

On the monkey poop that afternoon, there was great excitement as Beth read to us. There is so much about our new land that we do not yet know, and which we are most anxious to discover.

'Oh, listen, listen!' Beth exclaimed while we pulled coloured thread through fabric. 'In New Holland there are . . . *cultivated openings which have been made by the axe on the summits of some of the loftiest hills, and which tend considerably to diminish those melancholy sensations its gloomy monotony would otherwise inspire.*' Beth deepened her voice and tucked her chin firmly to her neck as she performed. She stood and began to pace the deck, pretending to stroke an imaginary moustache.

'*The weather in the month of May is truly delightful. The atmosphere is perfectly cloudless, and the mornings and evenings become with the advance of the month more chilly, and render a good fire a highly comfortable and cheering guest. Even during the middle of the day the most violent exercise may be taken without inconvenience . . .* How very fortunate, ladies! Exercise without inconvenience! That is what we require! And what else would you like to know?' She peered around at our faces, squinting as though from behind spectacles.

'About the vegetation, perhaps? Here: *There is no underwood, and the number of trees upon an acre do not upon an aver-*

age exceed thirty. They are, in fact, so thin, that a person may
gallop without difficulty in every direction . . .' Beth kicked
her feet in front of her.

'Gallop! Well!'

'Beth!' Matron looked up from the chicken coop where
she had been sleeping. 'Are you causing trouble?'

Captain Fryer's currents are drawing us south. Some time
ago when I looked into the ocean I saw an underwater garden. Billowing red flowers with fine tendrils drifting
slowly amongst luminous green beads. The flowers weave
independently, diving like seabirds. They are drawn to
others of their kind and they float through the water, a
string of deep red fir.

Perhaps the blood of women has tinted them dark.
There is something calming about their soft swimming.
Since it is no longer possible to capture wildflowers into a
colourful bunch, and sit them in a vase on my dresser, I
wondered if I could hold the underwater flowers in a jar on
the dining table. I asked Mr Hollyworth.

'Yes,' he said. 'I think I can bring you some seaweed.
And some water. But Sarah, the smell. Are you sure?'

That evening, Mr Hollyworth brought a pickle jar of
yellow water. I held out my hands and he reached into his
pocket, frowning. He dropped moist tufts into my hands,
smiled, and climbed the hatchway stairs. After he had
gone, the others crowded around to see what I had been
given.

Beth screwed up her nose. 'It's awful,' she said. The texture was rough; the seaweed was a fat clump on my palm. The green beads were punctured and torn.

'Oh Sarah, must you?' Eliza asked.

'What is that smell?' Annie asked from her bed, as the odour of warm salt drifted around the room.

'Put it in the jar,' Charlotte said. 'Let's see what happens.' She unscrewed the lid. The water rocked from side to side as though Mr Hollyworth had captured waves. I dropped the clump into the container. Slowly, the clump unwound and the tendrils began to fan outwards.

'Oh.' All the girls in my mess were standing around now, watching the seaweed like a shy animal feeling its way around the jar. We placed it underneath the lamp and the crimson glowed.

There is no relief from the heat, which is unlike anything I have known before. It is an unnatural heat and I feel as though I am too close to fire. Yet there is nowhere to run. The sea glows turquoise. It takes all our strength to keep from diving into the ocean.

One afternoon while Matron slept and we slumped on benches, I noticed that Charlotte was whispering. I turned to look at her face and saw that her eyes had fixed as though on the face of a companion sitting between us. I could not understand her words at all, and wondered if she was uttering words or simply opening and closing her mouth as dumbly as a fish. There was no one there. Her face dripped moisture and her hair, beneath her bonnet, was glued to her scalp. Suddenly her eyes fluttered wildly around the deck. She stood and ran towards the water. By the time I realised what she was doing, it was too late. I was two feet from Charlotte when she jumped overboard. It was my cry that aroused Matron. While she pushed me back towards my bench, I watched Charlotte's blue striped dress billow underneath the water. Her arms were out-stretched and her hair, escaping the bonnet, flowed around her. She looked as though she was flying. I was exhilarated at the sight of Charlotte floating so delicately beneath the water. I even thought, briefly, that I might join her. Then I realised that she was not coming to the surface.

Everything happened so slowly. The cry for help that came from Matron was like the whistle of a train that was running out of steam. The sailor who jumped from the rigging moved as though he were already beneath the sea. His body formed a neat arc as he dived into the ocean. I watched his strong arms in the water and his golden hair turn dark brown. Matron gasped as the sailor slipped his right arm around Charlotte's belly and pulled her towards air. There was a splash as they broke the surface of the water. Charlotte was limp already in the sailor's arms and his forehead was creased.

'Quickly!' he spluttered. 'Doctor . . .'

'Doctor!' one of the girls cried. Before long, everyone was shouting for Doctor Carpenter.

One sailor secured the rope ladder while another climbed half way down and helped lift Charlotte's sodden body onto the poop. As they laid her on the deck, Doctor Carpenter emerged from steerage, buttoning his shirt and blinking in the sunlight. Charlotte had lost her bonnet and her hair hung in dark, tangled strands around her face. Her top button had come undone, showing her smooth ivory neck.

'She's not breathing.' The sailor who had rescued Charlotte sounded as though he might cry. Doctor Carpenter pushed Beth aside and knelt on the deck next to Charlotte. We all gasped as he slid his fingers into her mouth.

'A jacket!' he called.

Someone threw him a heavy brown coat.

He then felt beneath her breasts and wrapped her lower chest in the coat before rolling her face downwards. Doctor Carpenter sat astride Charlotte's back and clasped her sides as though he was trying to fasten her to the poop. He rocked firmly backwards and forwards.

'I need to pump out the water,' he muttered, and water began to trickle from her mouth.

'She's moving,' someone whispered.

Charlotte's fingers twitched.

I was not sure whether I had imagined the movement.

'Garls.' Matron looked around at us and then fell silent.

Charlotte moved.

'Matron,' Doctor Carpenter turned to Matron as he stood. 'We need blankets and hot flannels; her limbs now must be rubbed warm. When she can swallow she must be given small quantities of warm coffee.'

At last Doctor Carpenter straightened his shirt and made his way to the captain's cabin.

While Charlotte lay still on her bed, Matron stuck mustard poultices to the soles of her feet. She lifted Charlotte's arms and placed one brick, covered in a flannel, under each armpit. I could see their sharp edges would bruise Charlotte's skin. Matron put a hand to her own forehead, closed her eyes and groaned. She pulled a small package from her apron and handed it to me.

'Sarah, I'd like you to apply smelling salts to Charlotte's skin and tickle her nose with a feather until she wakes.'

A little later I sat on Charlotte's bed, combing the salt from her hair.

'I saw McGovern,' Charlotte whispered when Matron had gone. 'In a fragrant garden beneath the sea. He beckoned to me; I wanted to be with him. The water was so refreshing, Sarah. It made me feel as though I was alive again.'

~

IN MY FIFTEENTH summer, Polly and I waited with nervous excitement for the boys to return once again. After I began to spend time with Richard, I had learned that I did not need to hide my thirst. Now I drank fifteen weak cups of tea every day until my body swam with fluids. Water made me feel strong. Mother faded almost to invisibility while I was swelling and throbbing to the tip of every finger.

Although Mother stared in disapproval, she did not say anything. Richard and I spent days in the Severn. He moved with the subtlety of a current, he fluttered like a sea breeze, his breath was sweet vapour. His eyes were deep pools and his skin glowed. He was moist to touch.

I do not believe it occurred to Mother or Father that I might love Richard. They would have taken steps to prevent it earlier. As it was, we were free to spend days in each other's company. Polly, William, Richard and I simply fell into two pairs. As we grew older, the four of us took long Sunday afternoon walks. William doted on Polly. She was small for thirteen and could ride his shoulders for miles; he would almost forget she was there. She made us laugh. 'Straight ahead, there's a good fellow,' Polly would say, playfully nudging our brother's side with the heel of her boot as she rode his shoulders. 'Look out, low clouds. I believe a storm is approaching!' She would hold her right hand over her eyes and squint, peering into the distance.

Richard and I came to know each other's thoughts without speaking. We walked and swam together. Sometimes I read him Coleridge in Father's library.

SOME TIME AGO the sailors celebrated the Dead Horse Ceremony. After hearing about the horse latitudes from Mr Hollyworth, we dreaded this. Matron said that all we needed to know about the ceremony was that it signified that the sailors had worked off the twenty-eight days that had been paid in advance before boarding the ship. I did not sleep for many nights as I thought about the lonely mare in her shed padded with horse fur. When Matron told us we were to stay below deck while the celebration took place, I became even more alarmed. It seems that whenever we are forced to remain below deck, the behaviour of those on board is so reckless as to endanger the safety of other passengers, and particularly the animals.

Matron herself went to the poop for the celebrations. Everyone was on deck apart from the unmarried women. We crowded beneath the hatchway stairs to hear what was being said. The riotous singing of the sailors became clearer as they neared the end.

> *'Poor horse, your time is come . . .*
> *Oh many a race I know you've won . . .*
> *He tried a Derby to win . . .*
> *Fetch plenty of tin . . .*
> *Mr Auctioneer, you can begin . . .'*

Another voice shouted, 'Bidding commences at five shillings, do I have a buyer . . . ?'

'Ten shillings.'

'One pound.'

'Six pounds.'

'Sold!'

There was much laughter as someone walked across the deck.

'No!' Annie muttered from the top of the hatchway stairs as she wrenched at the door.

Suddenly there was a loud splash and people cheered while more singing began.

'Poor old horse you're going to die . . .'

We made our way back to our beds and lay down in silence.

We were still morose the following morning when Mr Hollyworth arrived to help with breakfast. He had become more talkative during the last few days.

'Beth,' he asked, 'what's the matter? You all look as though someone has died.'

'The mare . . .'

'Oh, no!' he said. 'That was no real horse. It was the Dead Horse. No more alive than this dining table! Constructed from a barrel!' Mr Hollyworth laughed. 'The sailors made his mane from hemp and used gingerbeer bottles for his eyes. He was lashed to a box and drawn along Egyptian-fashion before being dropped into the sea.'

⁓

ONE CLOUDLESS AFTERNOON we were walking by the Severn when Polly suddenly became agitated. 'It's Mr Peterson,' she hissed. She struggled so quickly to get down from William's shoulders that Richard had to catch her to prevent her landing on the wet grass. I do not know how Polly recognised Mr Peterson from such a distance. He drew nearer, walking steadily and calmly, making no effort to hurry. We slowed as we neared him. It was as though we were trying to prevent the meeting.

'Good afternoon. Ladies.' He bowed. Polly muttered to her boots.

'Would you care to join us?' William asked him, staring curiously at Polly.

'Thank you.'

I walked ahead between Richard and William. Polly followed shyly, her arm linked to Mr Peterson's. He was asking her about music.

Mr Peterson made Polly quiet. Her eyes grew larger, deeper blue and more beautiful. She smiled more often but spoke less. 'Do you think you could love him, Polly?' I asked her one evening before we went to sleep. She blushed.

'He makes me feel safe,' she said.

Polly told me that William had been talking to her often about Mr Peterson. William wanted to know if he was good to her. 'He is my good friend,' William had said. 'But you are my sister and I do not want you to marry any man whom you do not like or who is not kind to you and does not always put your own considerations first.' I had thought that Polly's relations with Mr Peterson would distract William. But one Saturday afternoon he found me reading in the garden. He sat next to me on the bench.

William and I always had trouble conversing. I knew he was as fond of me as a brother should be of his sister, yet I rarely understood what he was really trying to say. On this occasion, he began by asking me about Mr Downing.

'He does not interest me,' I said. 'We have nothing to speak about.'

'But Sarah, he comes from a good family. He is a kind-hearted man. What is it that you dislike about him?'

'Nothing exactly. There is just nothing that I like.'

'Sarah, you know, there are some things that cannot be spoken; some people the laws of the bible and of morality forbid us to love in certain ways. There have been mistakes. Mother was misguided and she has repented for her sins . . . It was long ago but I have heard . . . Father, I believe, has forgiven. But you do know?'

I stared at his near-rectangular nose. 'Know what?' I asked him.

'Blood that should never—things that happened before you were born. Things best not spoken of, but things that must be understood. *Secrets*.'

The feeling that I thought was love made me tired. It made the skin on my arms tingle and it lightened my limbs. It carved a gentle smile on my face. It kept my mind awake during the night. I was always comfortable with Richard because in my mind we were never apart. Everywhere I went in sleep he came. We climbed mountains hand in hand. We built rafts and floated along the Severn in each other's arms. In my dreams Mother was happy that I had found a man I loved who would also be my husband; Father would give his blessing and his grandfather's bible. The life inside my head was more real to me than the walk to church and Sunday evening recitals for Mr Downing.

I do not know what love is supposed to feel like. I know that it is possible to live a lifetime in the arms of someone comfortable whom I do not love. I still do not know if I love Richard for the parts of myself that he enabled me to observe from a distance. It is perhaps too late to doubt that the love I feel is that of a wife for her husband.

My measurements were taken for a white dress. William started building me a trunk. Father began giving me secret winks and smiles, which were most uncharacteristic of him. Polly talked about flowers and candlelight. It was Florrie who made me realise it was time to act upon these changes when she said, 'I hope you will come and visit often, Miss.' I stared at her in surprise.

'Visit?'

'That nice young man, Miss . . .'

'Oh. Oh, I see. Yes!' I smiled and left the room. Sitting on my bed, I felt the walls begin to shake. They were moving in around me. I knew that soon there would not be enough air here for me to breathe.

On the night I left, I sobbed as I collected my last few possessions while Richard waited outside in the darkness. Together we had struggled to carry my trunk from the work shed where I had filled it with my belongings that afternoon. Now Richard waited with the trunk in Father's carriage. There was still time to wake Polly and tell her I was leaving. I ran to her room. She slept on her left side, the fingers of her right hand curled beneath her chin. Even in sleep she smiled. Polly slept in the same position as she had when she was three years old. I sniffed and held my right forefinger beneath my nose.

'Goodbye, Polly.'

'Goodnight, Sarah,' she whispered without opening her eyes.

～

TWO NIGHTS AGO I woke to hear Lydia sobbing. I climbed to her bunk and noticed that her face was damp.

'Lydia, you're sick. Let me tell Matron.' She clutched my hand and would not let me go.

'Sarah, help me. Please. Do not tell anyone.'

Her eyes were glazed and her fingernails dug into my skin. I climbed down from her bed to where the water jug was and found a flannel. I noticed Charlotte sit up in bed in alarm.

Charlotte and I sat with Lydia together through the night, holding her hands, stroking her face and trying to cool her with a compress. Lydia gasped and convulsed. At one moment when she lay almost still with her eyes closed, she said, 'Sing to me, Sarah.'

My voice shook and I could remember the words to nothing but 'Slap-bang, here we go again'. My voice was weak and I feared waking the other girls. I stopped. She was still and for a few moments I dared not move. Suddenly she reared up like a horse and gasped in pain.

'Sarah, sing something else.' I began softly to sing 'Christians Awake, Salute this Happy Morning', which grew louder as I neared the chorus. I was almost at the end when I noticed that Beth was walking towards the bed.

'What is it?' she hissed.

'Lydia—'

'Good Lord! I'm going to get Matron.'

Holding the lamp, Matron peered into the knotted bedclothes. Mr Hollyworth pulled off a blanket, while Doctor Carpenter dragged Lydia to the edge of her bed by the right leg. I saw blood. Lydia roared in pain.

'They will cure her,' I told Charlotte. Charlotte sobbed and ran back to bed.

The metal plates on the dining table began to take shape as the light spilled through the hatchway.

'Sarah.' Matron stared into my face as though she had not seen me before. 'I would like you to pack Lydia's possessions into her canvas bag so they can be taken to the hospital. She will not be returning for some time.'

I did not want to touch the bed that smelt so strongly of Lydia's sickness and blood. The tangled bedclothes could have contained a person. Later that morning, though, I folded the sheet, and shuddered when I noticed the large oval-shaped brown stain on the mattress. It looked as though someone had sliced her open and she had spilled.

'You know she was confined.' Beth lifted the pillow.

'Her name wasn't Lydia at all, it was Margaret. She left England without telling anyone. Mrs Peacock is caring for her baby daughter.'

The roughly sanded trunk was an untouched reminder of Lydia. I imagined smoothing it with my hands. If I rubbed it every day, my skin would coat it in an oil that would prevent the water getting in. The thought that someone would take it away filled me with panic. It was of some comfort to feel its sharp corners pushing into my shins as I rushed past.

I tried to open the trunk. Matron had not mentioned it and I wondered whether she had forgotten its existence. Charlotte had been eyeing it anxiously whenever she passed.

'Does it still belong to Lydia,' she whispered, 'now that she's dead?'

For other girls, the chest was a point of blindness. They learned to walk around it without hitting their ankles on its corners. They kept their eyes level with the ninth hatchway step. It was as though Lydia's body lay crumpled in the corner and no one knew quite what to do about it.

The trunk seemed to grow until it took up almost half our berth. I knew that if we did not clear it away, there would not be enough room for us in steerage. Our number of belongings always seems to increase. It is not possible that any of us have any more possessions than when we first boarded the vessel, yet we are being crowded out of our beds by handkerchiefs, stockings and pannikins. Tin plates and pickle jars have overflowed from the dining table into our beds. It is as though the objects multiply in their boredom. They climb out from where we have tried to hide them during the night. They long for softer surfaces that will not allow them to slide so easily with the motion of the ship.

I wondered if the objects in Lydia's trunk would tell me her secrets. Perhaps her life had been written on yellowed pages and fastened with a ribbon. I imagined a love token from the boy in the cemetery. A bent metal coin roughly engraved with the picture of a house constructed of tiny holes as though it might, at any moment, disintegrate. Or decorated with curled words of love that Lydia could have shown her child. A small piece of England for Lydia to give her daughter when she would have been old enough to understand homesickness. But the trunk was large. And it had been permitted in steerage where others had not. I climbed past the clutter and sat on the damp boards in front of the trunk. I stroked the lid. It was as sticky as honey. I gripped the front two corners and pushed upwards. Nothing happened.

'It's locked, Sarah,' Charlotte said. She handed me the knife and my hands began to tremble at our violence.

'There must be a key,' I said. 'Where is Lydia's bag?'

Finally, I wrote a short letter to Mrs Peacock. My fingers were so stiff that it was difficult to grip a quill. The motion of the vessel made my characters appear like jagged mountains. In the note I explained that we needed to clear out Lydia's trunk in order to distribute her belongings and to ascertain what should be given to her daughter. I asked if she could check Lydia's canvas bag to see if it contained a key. I gave the letter to Mr Hollyworth. For three days I waited.

The mystery of the chest was never far from my mind. There were times when I imagined it to be empty. There were other times when I thought it to be filled with dolls and tin soldiers. I liked the idea that it was loaded with books that Lydia had intended to use to establish her own library on arrival in the New World.

On the fourth day, Mr Hollyworth appeared with charred cabbage that Beth had prepared. Matron paced the berths of the unmarried women's accommodation, occasionally jerking her head to peer at one of the girls. She did not notice that Mr Hollyworth gave the charred cabbage to me instead of to Beth. As soon as Matron had passed our berth and moved on to the next one, I started poking the thick leaves with a spoon. Something scraped the bottom of the dish. When Matron had passed a second time, I closed my eyes and pushed my fingers into the steaming dish. The key was hot in my hand.

It was the following afternoon before Matron went to talk to Doctor Carpenter and we could think about opening Lydia's trunk. I wondered, suddenly, whether it was the right thing to do.

'What else could be done with it?' Charlotte asked.

'We could ask Mr Hollyworth to help us carry it up on deck and heave it into the ocean.'

Beth looked up from the dining table where she was squinting to see her stitching.

'We cannot get rid of the trunk without knowing what is in it,' she said.

'Whose trunk?' Eliza asked, looking up from her journal. 'Oh, I'm sure Lydia would not mind.'

I turned the key while Charlotte leaned over me and pushed up at the corners. The chest groaned and shuddered. The first thing I saw was thin white fabric. I could see now, how much better it would have been if there was enough room for all of our belongings in steerage where it was dryer than below. The white fabric was only slightly damp. Charlotte choked and a tear dripped from the end of her nose. I lifted the fabric. It was the bodice of a bridal gown. A lace collar fell to the boards. Even Beth was quiet as she gently lifted a flattened sleeve from the trunk. We found the entire gown in small pieces. The skirt was wrapped around a tin box. I handed it to Eliza. We all watched as she tugged at the lid. The lid did not budge.

'It's rusted,' she muttered. She slid a fingernail underneath and then pulled again, harder. The lid came away from the box with such force that it sent the contents soaring up into the air. Hundreds of patterned triangles were flung up towards cabin class. Wings caught the sea breeze and for the first time in months, they fluttered. For a few seconds we imagined ourselves to be in an exotic garden. We were surrounded by blue, crimson, orange and mauve. We were showered in butterflies.

There is now little difference between my days and my dreams. They are all filled with the lilting voices of girls. I wonder if I will ever again know the presence of true silence. There are too many lives to think about.

It had been several weeks since the vessel did anything other than occasionally rock ever so gently upon the water. But last night I was jolted from sleep by the roaring of the sea and thumping at the vessel. It sounded like a giant hammer was trying to smash her to pieces. In my dreams, the captain had been forcing the vessel to move more quickly than she was able and she began to tip. I was fully awakened by screaming.

People muttered prayers. Others shouted instructions to gather up belongings and children. There was great commotion on board. The ship heaved with such violence that I thought we would be flung to the deep. Waves crashed over the deck. I could feel spray spitting through the hatchway door.

Then, within a few minutes, the vessel became calmer.

This morning I heard that we experienced a tide-rip that carried us out of the calm belt in which we had been stranded for several weeks. The ship has begun to move once more.

Doctor Carpenter says that the calm belts on the ocean are like mountains and that it is necessary to find the gaps and passes and sometimes to advance high up their craggy surface in order to cross them. He says that there are real mountains beneath the sea and that islands are the visible peaks of immense ranges.

I wonder what the seabed would look like if we could empty her of water. I imagine warm sunlight shining over a skin of clouds. I imagine mountain thigh-bones and ridges of spine. Ribs tower above allowing shafts of sunlight to pass between them. Around me I see mountains of knee-caps. I curl comfortably into smooth hip-bones, blanketed and sheltered against the wind. Here I fall into a perfect sleep.

But in reality a deep uneasiness is working its way up through my ankles. On the poop this afternoon, I noticed that the wind is blowing thunder towards us. The clouds are thick; tinted dusty yellow and purple. Water hangs in the sky. The seabirds following the vessel are swept helplessly upwards.

In celebration of commencing the final stage of our journey, the captain has allowed some of the cabin-class men to play 'potting the floating hat'. The master has given the men the use of their weapons for an afternoon. The captain himself tied a sailor's hat to a line, which was flung overboard. The hat bobbed up and down and the men took turns in trying to shoot it. Of course, at the sound of the first shot, Matron sent us below deck.

We have hoisted our colours to another ship that is floating towards us. They have signalled back that they are going home. Everyone is trying to finish up letters now. Despite the heat and the rocking of the ship, they sit at the dining table like schoolgirls, writing so hard that their fingers cramp. I must try to write to my mother once more. It is so difficult to know where to begin. I do not know when we will next have an opportunity to send mail. I find the task impossible. What am I to say to any of them?

Mr Hollyworth collected coal from the galley and twine for us to anchor our letters with the coal. We were permitted on the deck and there was much scrambling as we rushed up the hatchway stairs to greet the passengers on the other ship. But we were disappointed to see the vessel bobbing up and down—and only a few sailors in sight. The ships rocking on the water were like elderly women conversing; nodding their heads out of time, one rising while the other falls, never quite meeting. Still the girls chattered and giggled. Matron could not make them quiet. They sat indelicately on the boards in the wind, tying their pages to coal.

When girls clutched two or three tiny scrolls and dangling pieces of coal, Beth began to shout. 'One . . . Two . . . Three . . .'

Hundreds of words flew up into the air. Black pellets rose upwards and showered the deck on the other ship, tumbling like rocks. I stood still, my eyes moist.

North of Antarctica
August 25, 1854

5. Mrs Louisa Garnett
c/- Frederick Garnett, Esq.
'Farraways'
Dorrington
Shropshire

My dear Mother,
     Please forgive me for what I have done . . .

MY HAIR IS matted like an old carpet and it no longer holds any pattern of neatness. I wear the uniform of the mad. It is stamped all over me in shredded dresses and sagging lips.

The right side of my body has slipped so far ahead that it has disappeared, leaving the left side behind. My head is frothing.

I fear that Cousin Richard is dead. It is long since I have seen him and I have no news. I fear he is weak with fever or that he has died and been committed to the deep. I do not know how I shall survive without him. It was never my intention to be alone.

I lie curled on my mattress. The familiar burning, aching and swelling reminds me of my womanhood. I whimper and long for warm hands to smooth the ache from my back. The ocean completes its cycle and flows from my body. Sometimes it is thin and spreads like bright paint. Sometimes it sticks to me in brown clumps. If I am limp there is less pain. I hum to the fish inside my belly to make him calm. Then he is still and I can try to sleep. He has become accustomed to my salt. I think he will always be inside me and I am glad to have shared my journey with him.

Strong winds are blowing us south and we are no longer allowed on deck. I shiver and sweat under my sheets; my feet are cramped with cold. Mr Hollyworth says there is snow and frost and that the risk of icebergs is great.

I no longer sense the passing of time. It may tick forwards when the vessel rocks east and backwards when it rocks west. Yesterday I heard a voice shout that the ship was wobbling like a drunken tailor with two left legs. I do not remember my age. I wonder if I will be wizened and hunched when we arrive in the New World. Or perhaps I will become a child again. Sometimes I hear the captain of our mess preparing food, or Matron asking Mr Hollyworth to take our meal to the galleys. At other times Matron says that we must be quiet for it is time to sleep. It is no longer dark only in the evenings. My body does not signal mealtimes.

I have a rising damp. It began in my toes and has started to move up through my chest. There is moisture quivering in my lungs. Sometimes my coughs are yellow and my sneezes glistening silver. There is a buzzing in my scalp. It does not hurt but tickles me while I sleep and I feel it throb underneath my fingers. It reminds me of my currents and I am glad they have not stopped flowing through my mind.

I have heard that sometimes the sea becomes so cold that vessels are swallowed by icebergs. Although the peaks of icebergs are sharp as needles, they grow from large round masses of ice that are shaped to float upon the ocean. I long to see bergs for I have heard that they can be as spectacular as palaces. Many a traveller has drowned with the satisfaction that her last sight upon the earth was one of glistening beauty before being pulled beneath the water while her soul was sucked up to the heavens along a path of ice. The size of icebergs beneath the surface of the sea is so unpredictably vast as to make them difficult to avoid.

There was a ship called the *Ocean Princess* whose hull became sealed within a frozen ball surrounded by a platform of ice that guided her towards the New World. Some of the cabin passengers held ice-skating balls there during the few hours of faint daylight while musicians played violins in a frenzy to keep warm. The vessel became a large island of ice that buffed it against bergs and cleared the way. It moved slowly but the sailors raised the shrouds and it inched towards the New World.

It was decided that a ball would be held. The cabin passengers spent much of the day preparing for the occasion. The women wore their most elegant gowns and covered themselves with shawls. They knew that they would have to dance all night for warmth. There was some trouble keeping the lamps alight, but a group of sailors devised a contraption from wood and canvas that protected two lamps from the wind. The cabin passengers skated mainly by moonlight.

This was indeed a grand ball. Even the captain attended,

leaving two sailors at the helm. Steerage passengers lined the rails to watch the festivities on the ice below. The musicians pulled greatcoats over themselves and, from the ship's deck, they played out of tune because their gloved fingers lacked precision and their ears were covered in woollen muffs knitted by the captain's mother, so they could not hear their own music. They kept time by watching the rhythm of the other musicians' bodies.

The cabin passengers passed bottles of gin around the platform of ice. They sang and shrieked in excitement. The celebrations would probably have lasted for days had everything gone to plan. But early the next morning, when the ice was slashed with cuts, the strings of the violins snapped and their bridges sprang into the sea. The platform of ice began to tear from the vessel.

People slipped and landed hard as they tried to run. The captain shouted instructions that everyone should move slowly and calmly. They should queue in an orderly fashion for the rope ladder. The first cabin passengers reached the ship. The gap of freezing water between the vessel and the ice was two feet and growing. Three people leapt towards the ship and were engulfed by the sea. Women wept as the island of ice floated back towards Old England. Some cabin passengers huddled together. Many could not bear to wait until their lungs were frozen. A number of men left their wives shivering in the middle of the island and slipped quietly into the water.

The musicians on deck stopped playing, looked at each other and with one movement, jumped down the hatchway stairs. The ship tottered for some time, and people in steerage screamed that the vessel was sinking. At daybreak word got out that the captain and almost all cabin passengers had indeed been lost.

The remaining sailors moved into the cabins and the steerage passengers slaughtered a pig. The sailors took turns guiding the vessel for the remaining journey. The matron allowed the unmarried women to bring up the trunks belonging to the cabin passengers, and there was much argument while gowns and jewels were distributed. The celebrations lasted almost until the vessel reached the New World.

I thought I should like to see snow falling on the ocean and wondered at the size of the flakes. Mr Hollyworth came to collect Beth's onion tart and I followed him, calling the pig, her bell echoing somewhere behind me, and carrying my birdcage, for I thought the animals should also like to see snowflakes. I did not remember to collect my boots or my cloak and no one noticed me leave as I climbed the hatchway stairs.

I barely reached the top of the stairs when the wind collected my skirts and sucked them to the splintered banisters. The cage swung in my hands while Artemis, Lares and Penates were blown from their perches. They huddled swollen together in a quivering mass of feathers when I opened the door of the cage. Flying ice stung my face and my hands were blotched crimson.

'You are free!' I shouted into the wind as I lifted the cage still higher. 'Go!' Lares and Penates were blown swiftly up into the air. They circled uncontrollably upwards and disappeared into a suffocating cloud.

I was shrouded by slippery fog and could not see the water. Immense palaces of ice with delicately carved external staircases stretched up into the sky. I walked towards a palace where a princess beckoned. As I drew nearer I saw that her neck was studded with garnets and she wore a deep blue gown. 'There is a fire burning in the hearth,' she told me, smiling. 'You will be welcome here. The cook is preparing a grand meal and we will play music throughout the night. There will be dancing and charades.' I wanted to run towards her but my limbs were frozen in place. The wind slashed my face and tried to force me back down the hatchway stairs but I would not be moved.

'I have found her!' Warm arms gathered my arms to my chest and carried me into darkness once more.

Sometimes I feel smooth hands stroking my forehead. I hear a sweet voice humming 'Do they miss me at home'.

We are thrown about on the ocean; I am woken when quick fingers tie my blankets to the boards so I cannot fall out of bed. I am stiff on my back and do not have the strength to change positions. People laugh as they mop the water that floods in from the water closet. My bed only gets a little wet, and this moisture is probably because I am leaking. My lungs cough mucus that tastes like blood. My mind is awash and I am all at sea.

It is dangerous to close my eyes, yet I lack the strength to open them. The tiny ocean roars beneath the bed. There is peace only for the few seconds that I manage to peel back my dry eyelids and stop trembling. I need to drag myself back from the panic of confusion. My mind is busy with noise and colour, hot and cold. I know that I am not in my own mess. It is always night outside my head. Instead of kicking Annie, I kick heavy blankets and stale air.

Lydia appears above my bed. I see her drifting through the hospital in her shawl. She is thinner than before. She strokes my forehead with fingers I cannot feel. Then she dips biscuits in blue treacle and holds them to my lips. The dryness of biscuits would soak up my blood. Lydia beckons me towards the hospital doorway and then fades. Somewhere on board ship, a child is screaming.

It is nearly the end. I have almost reached the place I will only be able to distinguish by the fact that it is *away*.

I wonder if everything will be upside down. I see trees with their roots sprouting up into the air. People wearing leather-lined hats on their heads and bounding upside down along cobbled streets.

Someone brings me a cushion stitched in bright colours. She assures me it is not stuffed with drowned women's clothing. It features an albatross soaring above a crimson ship. The sea underneath the vessel is a thin green line. The ship is trapped forever.

'But there is no wind.'

She laughs. 'There is plenty of wind, Sarah, but I could not show in my picture that the ship was moving. This ship is captured for you to keep. To remember the time you spent with us.'

'Have you any news of Richard?'

'Mr Hollyworth speaks little and we do not hear much at all.'

Someone else speaks. 'Sarah! Doctor Carpenter has sent you some wine and boiled carrots. Do try to eat.' My throat is too dry to swallow food. But liquid is poured into my mouth and warmth slides down inside my body towards my toes.

'I am going to eat with the captain this evening.'

I try to peer into her face but she is straightening my blankets.

After the rain I went for a walk in the woods with Richard. He ran ahead and shook wet branches, sprinkling my hair with droplets. He collected fresh wildflowers and held them out to me.

'Lullen Sady,' he said, handing me Sullen Ladies with smooth pink petals and wiry green stems. The flowers had golden hearts. I wore my yellow summer gown and my white bonnet. Richard told me of his plans to emigrate to New Holland. He had a friend in Sydney who wrote letters describing the beautiful landscape. The friend wrote that hard work was well rewarded there. The soil was moist and thick with nuggets of gold. Richard wanted to spend his days by the sea. Even though he would soon own his father's cottage in Shropshire, he knew this would not be enough for him to live comfortably. Although Uncle Frederick wished him to go to Cambridge, Richard had little inclination to continue his studies. He gave me the flowers and put his arm through mine. I grew tired and stopped to rest on a tree stump. He sat in the moist clover at my feet and took my hand. I felt the wetness of his palms.

They say it is very cold and people are making fire baskets to hang from the beams. The hospital glows green, orange and mauve. The smoke makes my eyes itch and water, even when they are closed. Crimson soot scatters like dust.

'I have such a headache. Do you mind if I take some of this?' A girl is sitting on my bed chewing a biscuit and holding a small bottle. 'Sarah, did you notice that the ship gave a horrid jolt last night? Cranky Jim is angry with me because I pitched a bucket of dirty washing water into his bed after he told Matron I was up on the poop during the night. Last night it was Cranky Jim's turn to steer the ship while the captain rested, and he tried to run the vessel into an iceberg to punish me!'

Richard came to speak to Father. Mother greeted Richard in the drawing room. I noticed her shudder as mud dropped from his boots. She looked into his face and was pleased to see him. Now that he was almost grown, he frequently stayed with his father, who worked in London. 'You will stay to supper this evening?' she asked. She told me that he looked like Uncle Frederick. When Richard asked Father for my hand, Father laughed.

'Come, come, Richard. Sarah is like a sister to you. Surely you cannot be serious.'

The ship creaks and groans. I am dizzy, I clutch my

mattress. When I am flung from my bed, I lie like a dead fish on the boards until someone lifts me. My skin is as pummelled as mutton beaten with a cleaver.

The smoke makes me cough. Salt water drips from my face. Someone is shrieking; others are shouting orders to fill buckets with water. I hear the roaring fire in Father's library. My eyelids are sealed to my face. I am sure the skin will tear when I force them open.

The fire is writhing like an eel along the beams. The flames glow green and scarlet. I close my eyes and imagine I am running. My limbs are heavy as stone.

'My very own maiden.' Mr Downing tried to smile but I saw a snarl on his face. I thought of the clothes-horse in my room that Florrie liked to call the *maiden*. Then I remembered Father's stories of Old Scotland and how a *maiden* had been used to behead criminals. I smiled to myself.

Water drenches my face and arms. I gasp for air. Somewhere a woman is in hysterics, screaming 'I do not want to die!' I can feel bodies rushing past me as someone shouts, 'The ship is going down! They are getting out the life boats!' People all around me beat their fists against the door and the wooden walls. 'They've fastened the hatches!'

Mr Downing's hands were clasped around my waist and I could not pull free. He trembled and his face was crimson, his lips tight over mine. I could not breathe and feared I would drown in his air.

'Father, I am going to marry Richard!' I screamed at him and he gripped my arm.

'You will do no such thing. You must go to your room now and read the Table of Kindred and Affinity. It is forbidden in the scriptures and in our laws for you to marry your—cousin.'

I sobbed in my bedroom for three days. My prayer book sucked the moisture from my hands. The red skin on my palms began to crack. I read my prayer book and could not find in the table any law against marrying a cousin. I could not bear the thought of being parted from Richard. On the fourth day I locked myself in the music room where I beat the pianoforte with burning fingers. I could not touch my violin for fear of snapping the strings and splintering its belly.

When Mr Downing and Mr Peterson came to supper on Sunday evening, I upset Mother by playing the *Grave* movement of Beethoven's *Pathétique* sonata and not saying a word.

'Something a little more cheerful and sedate perhaps,' Mr Downing suggested when I had finished.

The night before I left, my mother sobbed without tears. 'Sarah, you must not ask me to explain. You have upset your father. Please understand that we cannot allow you to marry one who is as close to you as a brother.'

I am trying not to blink my eyes for fear they will seal shut again. A woman is hunched in a corner. She sobs over an infant, her hair dripping in its face. The elderly man in the bed next to mine is shouting 'Stop this at once!' at the beams. A sailor is kneeling beside his bed praying. The room is grey with smoke. Those with any strength at all are standing, a motley collection of crinkled nightgowns, near the hatchway.

We took the steam train to London. Uncle Frederick's cottage was walled with books. We sat by the fire and I watched flakes falling from his scalp into his cake. His face was as dry as paper to touch.

'Goodbye, Father.' Richard had shaken his father's hand. He had not wanted him to become suspicious, he told me afterwards.

'I must take Sarah home, but I will visit you again next week.'

'Dear Sarah,' Uncle Frederick smiled wistfully, touching my cheek. 'How you resemble your mother! Give her my regards, won't you?'

I see us arriving at Birkenhead some time before we were required to report. A guard at the station allowed us to leave our trunks in a back office.

'Collect 'em before dark, mind,' he told us. Richard took my hand and led me from the station. We had not walked very far when we saw the water.

'There she is,' Richard smiled. 'The Maiden Tide.' The vessel glimmered in the morning sunlight, rocking on the water. She was shining white. I was surprised at her small size; I had expected a floating castle. I turned and saw the ocean in his eyes.

'What is a *maiden tide*?' I asked.

'One that has not been torn by vessels entering or leaving the dock.' Richard frowned. 'The vessel will be safe,

Sarah. She is strong and solidly built. She will carry us safely to our new land.'

We stood silently, staring at the sea. Richard turned to me and tugged at the fair hair that hung down my back. 'Such lovely maiden hair,' he smiled.

'Take some,' I said. 'To remember me . . .'

'But Sarah, I—'

'Cut it. You have your knife . . .'

I clamped my eyes shut and held my hands over my ears while he pulled out his knife. I barely felt him slice off the ends of my hair. When I opened my eyes I realised that they were moist with tears.

At Birkenhead, each girl was an island in a sea of dust. I could feel the roughness of my trunk despite layers of petticoat beneath my skirts. William had not yet completed sanding the wood when Richard helped me take the trunk from the wood shed out into the darkness. My fingers were lumps of skin embedded with splinters.

'Have you a pocket-handkerchief?' I asked a girl next to me as my eyes began to water and my nose twitched.

'Not one I'd like to give you!' she retorted, pointing her sharp nose to the ceiling.

Others did not weep for dead music. They wailed for lost siblings and a perilous voyage. For frail parents and solid friends. I did not wish to speak to them. I could not bear to know their stories.

I feel as though I have been washing in my nightdress. I can no longer see any flames.

'Calm yourselves!' Doctor Carpenter is standing in the doorway.

'We have had a small fire, but it has been put out. Please go back to your beds.'

Someone is pulling me to a sitting position while another person lifts the wet nightdress over my head. A clean nightdress is pulled over my arms.

'Where is Richard?' I ask.

'Hush, now.'

When they have left me alone I sneeze droplets of black soot onto my sleeve.

The feeling on board the vessel has changed. Sometimes wild singing emanates from the poop. It sounds as though they are sanding the decks now, and will soon be painting them for our arrival. There is a new emptiness inside me.

Eliza is strong again I think, and comes to visit every day. She brings black tea that dries my throat, and food from the saloon table. I seem to be able to eat a small portion of macaroni soup and jelly pudding. How strange to have a flavour other than sickness in my throat. Eliza says there is to be a final dance for the unmarried women. I cannot imagine ever dancing again. She has given me paper. Is it to begin making decorations? I tear a square of paper into a long chain and I wrap it in folds around my neck.

'Eliza, please tell me what has happened to Richard.'

'I have heard nothing Sarah, but I will ask the captain at dinner. I have been permitted to sit at his table, you know. Since you have been so ill, perhaps he will allow you to see Richard once again. But quiet, now. Your fever is high.'

I can no longer sleep during the day and I long to be back with the others. In the ship hospital the elderly man in the bed next to mine is dead. Doctor Carpenter says it is only a matter of days now, until I can be back with my Dunkeys. I think he laughs. Soon I will be strong enough to write to my mother.

In my mind now I am standing on a beach staring out to sea. The sand is soft between my toes. I am pleased not to be moving with the ocean. My hair is loose, blowing around my face. My dress quivers in the wind and I feel strong once more.

The water is a rippling creature of jelly that laps softly at my feet, stretching its moist tongue to lick my toes. I no longer feel its wet caresses. The sun shines all the way to the golden sand on the seabed. Jagged reflections of water paint scales beneath the sea. The sea is tinted jade and draws me towards it. The tide whispers, 'Sarah. Sarah. Sarah . . .'

But I am now free to move onwards. I walk past the sea and wonder at how tame it appears from land. How mild is the ocean when the wind is gentle. How unhaunted by its own reflection.

An albatross flies overhead and I do not wonder that it chooses the ocean over which to fly. It moves inland and I turn to watch its flight.

I am folding a piece of paper into a rose when I notice a ragged figure with a face like mine, wandering towards me.

He sits with me now and we tell each other stories of our voyages on this ship. He pinches my wrist and tells me that stories shall spill from my eyes. Tomorrow he will bring paper and ink to begin writing all this, at last, to my mother.

I will pack the letter into my tin box and seal it in a watertight container. We intend to attach a hollow ball with a small chain to enable the box to float. Richard says he will drive a broomstick through a bunghole and pitch the tin box overboard. We expect it to float to the Brazils in two days.

ACKNOWLEDGEMENTS

THE SALT LETTERS began as an Honours thesis in the English Department at the University of Melbourne.

I am grateful to Lionel Bradshaw for showing me Louisa Cobden's letter to her daughter Sarah, which provided the inspiration for my book. The intricacies of Sarah's character and story are fictitious.

I have relied on a large number of primary and secondary sources dealing with early emigration to Australia. In particular, I am indebted to the work of Dr Andrew Hassam for bringing many journals of early Australian immigrants to my attention. Both the diaries themselves and Andrew's commentary on them were very important in providing idioms and incidents which I wove into my text. Without the original voices of these early immigrants, my novel could not have been written.

I have drawn on certain primary sources. The sections on pages 60 and 141 are directly quoted from the *Book of Common Prayer* (Edinbugh: Adrian Warkins, 1756). M.F. Maury's book *The Physical Geography of the Sea and its Meteorology* (London, 1861), written in highly evocative language, gives a varied picture of nineteenth-century attitudes towards the ocean. I have used the first verse of 'A Sailor's Adieu' (from *A Garland of New Songs*, Newcastle-upon-Tyne) on page 133. The Dead Horse Ceremony on pages 153 and 154 is taken from George H. Haswell's *Ten Shanties on the Australian Run, 1879* (Mt Hawthorn: Antipodes Press, 1892). The passages on pages 146–147 are indeed from Wentworth, W.C. Esq.: *Statistical, Historical and Political Description of The Colony of New South Wales and Its Dependent Settlements in Van Diemen's Land* (London: G. & W.B. Whittaker, 1819). Cures for various illnesses, as well as recipes will be recognisable to some readers as having been taken from *The Book of Household Management* (London: Ward, Lock and Tyler, 1861) by Mrs (Isabella Mary) Beeton.

An exhibition of convict love tokens at Hyde Park Barracks Museum in Sydney in 1998 provided great insight into the ways in which people remembered departed loved ones in the nineteenth century. The re-creation of steerage conditions at the South Australian Maritime Museum, Port Adelaide, aided my own descriptions of the experience of extended sea travel.

Much important work, particularly in the planning stages of my book, was completed while on a mentorship program funded by the Australia Council at Varuna Writers' Centre in the Blue Mountains. I would like to thank Peter Bishop for his relentless enthusiasm, and encouragement. I would also like to thank Brenda Walker, my mentor, for her insight. I was fortunate in having the opportunity to return to Varuna and take part in an editorial mentorship. I am grateful for Judith Lukin-Amundsen's creative and sensible editorial guidance. I also appreciate my agent Fran Bryson's continuing support.

Many people have assisted me with the writing of this book. I would particularly like to thank: Golda Schoenbaum, who recognised that it was a novel before anyone else did; Natasha Tsykin, Kate Macdonell, Rupert Smith, Vanessa Griffiths and Gill Barnsley, who gave time out of busy lives to read numerous drafts. Finally, I would like to thank my parents who understood that this was something I had to do.

SELECT BIBLIOGRAPHY

Beeton, Mrs (Isabella Mary): *The Book of Household Management* (London: Ward, Lock and Tyler, 1861)

Charlwood, Don: *The Long Farewell* (Melbourne: Penguin Books, 1981)

Church of England: *The Book of Common Prayer* (Edinburgh: Adrian Warkins, 1756)

Hassam, Andrew: *No Privacy for Writing: Shipboard Diaries 1852–1879* (Melbourne: Melbourne University Press, 1995)

Hassam, Andrew: *Sailing to Australia: Shipboard Diaries by Nineteenth Century British Emigrants* (Melbourne: Melbourne University Press, 1995)

Haswell, George (ed.): *Ten Shanties: Sung on the Australian Run, 1879* (Mt Hawthorn: Antipodes Press, 1892)

McCrae, H. (ed.): *Georgiana's Journal* (Sydney: Angus & Robertson, 1934)

Marshall, J. (printer) *'The Sailor's Adieu' in A Garland of New Songs* (Newcastle-upon-Tyne)

Maury, M.F.: *The Physical Geography of the Sea and its Meteorology* (London, 1861)

Smith, Bernard: *Imagining the Pacific in the wake of the Cook Voyages* (Carlton: Melbourne University Press at the Miegunyah Press, 1992)

Waite, Vincent: *Shropshire Hill Country* (London: Dent, 1970)

Wentworth, W.C. Esq.: *Statistical, Historical and Political Description of The Colony of New South Wales and Its Dependent Settlements in Van Diemen's Land: with a particular enumeration of the advantages which these colonies offer for emigration, and their superiority in many respects over those possessed by the United States of America* (London: G. & W.B. Whittaker, 1819)

CHRISTINE BALINT was born in Melbourne in 1975. Her work has appeared in *Australian Short Stories, New Writing Magazine*, and *The Best Australian Short Stories 1999. The Salt Letters* is her first novel and was shortlisted for the Australian/Vogel Literary Award. Christine Balint is studying for her Ph.D. in Creative Writing and teaches at Melbourne University.